BLAZE PASCAL

and

the Courage of Being

BLAZE PASCAL

and
the Courage of Being

An Epic Novel By

KENNETH D. STEPHENS

Adelaide Books
New York / Lisbon

2018

Blaze Pascal and the Courage of Being
An Epic Novel
By Kenneth D. Stephens

Copyright © 2018 By Kenneth D. Stephens

Published by Adelaide Books, New York / Lisbon

Cover design & Interior Formatting:
Adelaide Books DBA, New York

Editor-in-Chief
Stevan V. Nikolic

For any information, please contact Adelaide Books
at info@adelaidebooks.org
or write to
Adelaide Books
244 Fifth Avenue, Suite D27
New York, NY, 10001

ISBN13: 978-1-7320742-9-3
ISBN10: 1-7320742-9-1

Printed in the United States of America

I

Once an old soul
lived in Contemplation,

a satellite city of the City of Angels near
the desert and the mountains and the sea.

From his cottage small and spare
he lifted his eyes to the hills
and saw Mount Contemplation,

which rose to the north in
the San Gabriel Range, his

humble abode set among
oak and jacaranda trees,
bougainvillaea and cedars,

myrtles and mesquite to the east,
pines and palms to the west,
watered by mountain streams.

His days were made pleasant
by mocking birds, bluejays,
robins, falcons, towhees,
eagles, and hummingbirds.

Daily he walked to the village and the
university, and up to the seminary
and the Garden of Ancient Trees,

where deep-toned chimes wafted on
ocean breezes from verandahs nearby.

The thin man wrote verses
every day and would say

things like, All flesh is grass,
and how life flies by at
downhill skateboard speed.

Why only yesterday
I was but a boy in
missionary boarding schools
in the Himalayas.

His speculations about being itself
rose from his own experience of life,

how the powers and particles
seek higher and higher ground,
yes, higher and higher ground,
against the waters of nonbeing,

how sapphires and fiery suns,
pale moons and diamond rings,

ballooning through space,
clustering and colliding,

are epiphanies all of
the courage of being.

And how in a billion light years the
powers and particles by secret strife

give birth to life and
the fight for freedom,
freedom from fear,

freedom from a life
with no meaning,
with no love or
opportunity to
learn and create.

II

Such was the brief ontology of the
old man who walked on the streets of the
town-gown city of trees and Ph.Ds,

stepping aside for running students,
and recalling the pain of his rushed
relationships of times now long gone,

relationships ruined, he said,
by how dumb he was, and which
left him dented, like his old but
beautiful blue Ford convertible.

Things about himself
still troubled him and
sobered his poetic lines.

He was a romantic soul.

He cried at the movies during scenes
of love found or love snatched away,

and when he heard songs like
Every Night in My Dreams,
You Look Wonderful Tonight,

and even old campfire songs like
Down by the Old Mill Creek
and especially Red River Valley.

His heart melted in La La Land
when Emma Stone sang,

Here's to the ones who dream,
foolish as they may seem.
Here's to the hearts that break,
here's to the mess we make.

III

It was the noontime meal
at the Ground of Being,

when the old soul's philosophical path was
obstructed by the giant man from Geneva,

a professor at the Sorbonne, known for his
classical work in atheism and Christianity.

He was here for a meeting of
the World Council of Churches.

Tall and heavy, with suit and tie,
and the air of authority as world
representative of the Protestants,

Anglicans, Baptists, Methodists,
Presbyterians, Lutherans, and
all the Reformed communions,

and all configurations of these
worldwide, historic and recent.

He stood looking down upon the old soul
in the middle of the dining hall and two
hundred and fifty people finishing lunch.

My question had sounded lunatic,
said the old soul later. I had
babbled for a faith common
among all sea-washed shores,

a humanity common beyond
the religions that divide us.

The man looked upon me knowingly,
and said quite emphatically, This is
an era of fragmentation and identity.
Just that, and he was whisked away.

Fragmentation and identity!
Fragmentation and identity!

The old man was undone by the big man's quick reply
and the sudden manner his question was dispatched.

That very evening at the theological seminary a
different conference of the religions was concluding.

The hall was a plush amphitheater
with soft carpet and seats, and filled
with seminary students and professors
and retired religious professionals.

The six panelists were arranged
behind long tables on the stage.

The Christian, Muslim, and Jew sounded
tight-lipped, premeditated, and defensive.

The Hindu and Jain leaders,
their words inspirational and
fluent like mountain streams,

unencumbered by belief system,
unburdened by institutional bias,

chided the talk of boundaries by the
scholars of the Abrahamic religions.

Their tone was urgent:
Hear the world calling,
Freedom now!
Freedom now!

Hear the youth chanting,
Give peace a chance!
Give peace a chance!

War is not safe for
children and animals!

Imagine no religion!
No hell below us!
Above us only sky!

IV

The next day he pondered these things,
composing verses in his head while
striding precariously from rock to rock
in Contemplation Creek in the mountains.

The man from Geneva had not commented
on the value of fragmentation and identity,
just the fact that it was the drift of the times,

but the old man had stood at the microphone last night
strongly pleading for a common faith, a world theology.

To which the Muslim scholar
had said a categorical NO!
and the old man thought
he heard a martial voice.

To which the Jewish rabbi also had said,
Our faith is a necessity for us. We are
surrounded by our Muslim neighbors.

And to which the Christian scholar had said,
But particularity is prior to universality.

What the Christian said gave him pause:

How dare you, old soul, he said to
himself as he straddled the rocks, how
dare you question your historicity
and deny the verses of your birth!

Yet those very verses, he replied, his
arms stretched outward for balance,

decry the noisy gongs and clanging cymbals
of loveless tongues and heartless creeds,

and call us to dwell instead on
whatsoever things are true,
whatsoever things are honorable,

whatsoever things are just,
pure, lovely, and gracious.

They call us to
embrace love as
greater than faith,
greater than hope.

If there is any excellence,
anything worthy of praise,
think on these things first.

Must we not leave the old country behind and
rise toward the heavenly city of universal truth?

Is not our ultimate identity,
our final resting place, where
we lay our burdens down,

on the banks of the mystical river, the
beautiful, the beautiful river, that flows
from the eternal snows of being itself?

Massive boulders blocked his climb.
Chaparral the color of cougars and coyotes
loomed, lanced, and leaped around him.

V

The Whitney Museum poster, the
Kienholz Back Seat Dodge 1938,

high on an old building
near Figueroa and Wilshire,

stared down on the street with
the final word on addiction.

Motorists avoided entrancement by it,
or even trying to comprehend it, an
impossibility, they knew, in city traffic.

Enough to keep your eyes on
the vehicles in front of you,
the vehicles behind you,
the vehicles beside you,

the vehicles coming toward you,
the vehicles crossing or turning,

the homeless, the intoxicated, and
the mentally ill on the crosswalks,
the lights, and the bicycles.

Pedestrians looked up,
hesitated, and moved on.

What they saw,
or thought they saw,
would take time.

Perhaps tomorrow we will
pause, if Metro is on time,
to make out the forms
and try to understand.

Right there under the poster,
in the well-known club
in the tall old building,
the old man loved Sahara.

VI

He had taken the elevator down,
walked past the life-size Buddha
to the cashier's desk, and
paid the entrance fee of $16.

He was standing there absorbing the
situation, the well-lit Chinese art,

silken hangings with dragons,
octopuses, naked women, the
surf of tsunamic ocean waves,
flowing sleeves of seaweed,

the Connie Francis oldie
Where the Boys Are,

the dancing girls chattering,
sitting on flowery couches,

the male customers waiting
at the counter and the tables,

the Chinese cashier, the waitresses,
and the Goldfinger sumo strongman,
one of the several security guards,

when Sahara, smiling brightly, came
walking toward him from the
dance floor area with a young man.

She was preppy and pretty, and
after the young man paid the
cashier, the old man by instinct,

trusting that she was right
for him, asked her to dance.

The dance floor and television rooms were separated
from the entrance area by screens and tropical plants.

In the dim glow he reached for her
as if he was reaching for his own life.

The music was American and British, from
Nat King Cole to Adele and Elton John.

He told her the part about philosophy
and was vague about his religiousness.

Best she not know of the
black academic robe
he'd wear in the pulpit,

given to him by Orielle Hoffmeister, a
church member many moons ago and
retired dean from Columbia University,

or the stole the many colors
of a Guatamalan clothesline

gifted to him by a search
committee long, long ago.

She had had a course in
existentialism she said
as they were dancing.

In his mysticism she felt his hunger.
In his philosophy she read his love.

She knew his soul in
the way he held her.

In her womanliness he felt her restraint.
In her youthfulness he knew that
she knew, but did not know she knew.

VII

He was with her less than an hour.
He tipped her, paid the cashier,
and took the elevator up, putting
the dancing quickly behind him.

Other men were waiting.

The Things We Did Last Summer
was the song playing as he left.
He had loved that song in college.

Bejewelled towers soared
into the misty, misty night.

It looked down upon
him in the parking lot,
the lighted Kienholz
Back Seat Dodge 1938,

a tableaux of sex in the old car,

beer bottles strewn
within and without,

the figures made of flock,
plaster cast, chicken wire,
polyester resin, and fiberglass.

The old man would tell no one
of Sahara and the Chinese club,
recently renamed The Abyss
because it sounded contemporary.

VIII

The old soul's lust diminished:
Fewer were the times he visited
the Metropolis of Angels just

to know the black crepe dress,
the silken dress of deep dusk blue,
and the contours he loved to touch.

Old soul philosopher at the end,
young soul student at the beginning:

There was no depth,
and no common cup.

And all the men were waiting.
And all the men were waiting.

She knew of existentialism,
but of Ain't Misbehaving
what could she do but
look away at the wall?

Abide old man abide. Why
mention the Arab Spring?

Why Muhammad Bouazizi, the
Tunisian vendor burning himself,
beaten and humiliated by the police?

Love had come as a stranger and
had grown around him as danger,

an Alcatraz of consequences,
surrounded by the sharks of envy
and the rapid currents of desire.

The false gods of
physical attraction,
surface beauty,

groundless love of
the addictive mind,

they waited like vultures
on the prison walls
for the victim to weaken.

Only the Kienholz of
the Whitney Museum
of American Art,

looking down on him
in the parking lot,
said I understand.

Only the Kienholz
Back Seat Dodge
said I understand.

IX

Release came not of his own:
Sahara disappeared from the Abyss.

Joy came in the morning:
He saw the sacred truth

of Sakhyamuni Buddha
and of John of the Cross

sail lightly away in a raft in the
great red sea of eastern clouds,
having done its work in a dream.

In the dream he was standing
on Vulture Ridge, looking
down on the Magic City
and the islands in the sea,

when he heard the voice from
the river on the north side
of Vulture Mountain saying,
Choose the middle path,

the path of the poor in spirit,
of radical spiritual humility,

the practice of deep thought,
detachment, transcendence,

which lead to freedom,
wholeness, and
the love of wild places.

The old man kept waking
and falling asleep, the
dream falling into segments
and coming together again,

with people expressing different
opinions about the voice, some saying
it was of John the Baptist, others of
Jesus, of Krishna, or of the Buddha,

most shrugging off the voice as
a projection of the human mind,

and people quarreling about the river
on the north side of Vulture Mountain.

Was it a version of the Jordan?
Was it a version of the Ganges?

Many voices were intruding,
some from the distant past,
some friendly, some hostile.

Now the old soul was in Platonic
Coffee at University and Church,

the old hippie cafe with wooden counters,
tables, chairs, and ceiling, featuring a wall

painting of John Lennon at the piano, and
posters of Brando, Bogart, and Bergmann.

He was listening to the 1970s
recording of Ringo Starr
singing You're Sixteen,
barely audible above the noise,

You come on like a dream,
peaches and cream,
lips like strawberry wine,

and looking out from his perch
at the counter upon the people
sitting at tables with their pets,

a young female boxer, a
Labrador poodle, a baby pit
bull in the arms of a student,

the interaction between these
and other pets passing by,

and the long line of suited
bicyclists, student couples
with their roller skateboards,
and families with their children.

A four-year old girl noticed the old man
watching and cried out, Who are you?

The noise in the cafe seemed to drop,
and her mother tried to hush her and
move her along in the line, but he

answered, quite embarrassed,
I am Blaze, Blaze Pascal, and
the noise rose again to normal.

The old soul awoke in a
sweat and sat up in bed.
The sun had not yet risen.

X

His real name was not Blaze Pascal,
only his secret name for himself.

He remembered his father talking of the
seventeenth century French mathematician,
scientist, philosophical theologian named

Blaise Pascal, whose
writings on
life and death,
mind and body, and
faith and reason

had been the subject
of his father's
doctoral dissertation.

The old man was a teenager then, and he was reading
Zane Grey westerns, Captain Marvel and the other
super hero, Robin Hood, and Flash Gordon comics,

once sending the cleaning man with
money to the English bookstore to buy
a certain Scandinavian nudist magazine
for him, and asking him to tell no one.

It was when he was in his early twenties
and in seminary in America, and his
ego was outstripping his puny mind-body,

that when the dean called him and joked about the
kinship between Blaise Pascal and Flash Gordon,

he emerged as Blaze Pascal in
the fecund tumult of his soul.

XI

That very evening Blaze Pascal was
in Dr. Josiah W. Harshorne's living
room at the Ground of Being, where
the tall man Martin Grablowski,

the wisest of mortals,
a church-going man,

said softly, almost in whispers as always,
We must protect our freedom while we can.

No one heard the evangelical's words,
drowned out they were by the loud egoism
common in the kingdom of deprived souls.

The environmental activists and scholars
were anxious themselves to be heard.

Blaze Pascal put down Grablowski's
words on his scratch paper of verses.

XII

It was Friday night and busy at
Main and Sixth in the Creative City.
Blaze was stopped at the light.

Hovercrafts rose like monster birds from
high buildings, and spotlights pierced the
apartment, industrial, and hospital areas.
City and corporate towers rose around him.

The homeless with their makeshift shelters
and carts with bottles and cans in plastic bags
were visible in the parks and on the streets.

A Hispanic family walked in a
crosswalk one by one in a line,
mother, father, grandmother,
children, and baby in a crib.

Do they have a place under the towers?
A good friend in the anonymous city?

The questions arose in his melting heart,
and then and there he breathed a prayer,

I myself am an immigrant.
I was on a visa, and as a

student my mind flowered
and reached for the beauty
and the controversy of life.

I did not have roots here,
I dared not fall short. And
when I fell short, there

were always certain magi
who dreamed a dream for
me and showed me the way.

We are the magi now, and we shall
dream dreams and show them a way,
all who seek food, water, sanctuary.

We shall meet them at the border,
where the barbs reflect the
silver light of the rising moon,

where there is surveillance for
drugs and human cargo, and the
products that move by sea and
above and under the ground.

Helicopters fly overhead.
Armed guards examine your
papers behind glazed windows.

At the border there is danger.
At the border there is a fearful
inhuman landscape of sadness.

And the border is the site
of many stories of danger.

Some day I'll sing my song,
adapted from the original in
the 1949 Streets of Laredo,

starring William Holden,
MacDonald Carey, Mona
Freeman, William Bendix.

I was in Ambala when I
saw the movie, for which
I had waited a long time,

because the photos had
been up for months in the
Air Force base theater.

Some day I'll sing my song,
I was just rambling through
on the streets of Laredo.

I was just a stranger that day
on the road to anywhere....

She was just rambling through....

We cried when we whispered manana.
We knew that soon we'd be parting.
We said I go back Santa Ana,
and she to Ol' Mexico....

XIII

That evening Blaze entered Club Zero,
which was at street level, and unlike the
Abyss in cultural and ethnic ways too.

Blaze stood with mainly Hispanic
men of every social class,
both young and old, and some

Chinese, Japanese, Philippinos,
Iranians, and African Americans,
all who could pay the $21 fee.

The only gringo he saw, apart
from some Russian women,
was an older man with a cane,
trimmed white beard, and hat.

This was also an old club and had
gone through changes of ownership.

The busy cashier's desk was not on
the far side from the entrance now.
It was there where you entered that
you paid the entrance fee as well.

The current cashier was a
Hispanic lady of his age.

He recognized her from a club
that had been closed down.

Cordial at first to see him, she
had grown resentful of his dancing
with the attractive young women.

The tables, chairs, and benches,
the old photos of movie icons,
of which Gary Cooper's was
by far the one he liked the most,

the antique chandeliers, the dance
floor, the sitting area for couples,
the TV room, and all the artwork
were still the same as in the 'sixties.

All the men were waiting for the one dancer
to appear, who would be chosen by the heart.

Could she be with a man behind the veil?
Could she be coming with the next shift?

Blaze himself had someone in mind, an
athletic, attractive woman in her late
twenties, her shoulder-length midnight
hair hanging loose, scattered, casting

a seductive look at him, dressed in a
white blouse and loose-fitting emerald
skirt with white swirls of ocean surf.

But he saw Sergio, the well-dressed
stocky fortyish Hispanic man ask

her first as he entered. Blaze and he
had talked at the counter in times past.

All Sergio wanted was to squeeze
information out of him about his
experience with the dancing girls.

Blaze gave him no such information.

It had happened before, Sergio and
he in competition for the one woman.

This woman was among the
most popular starlets here.
Again he had come too late.

He sat down at a table
wondering about her.
Did she have children?
Did she have another job?

Did she speak English?

Live with her parents?
Was she from Mexico?
El Salvador? Honduras?
Was she divorced?

The salsa and the rock had him
shaking and tapping his shoes.

People watched his shoulders arch, weave, roll,
saw him dream deliriously out loud and in love.

And when the Ringo Starr hit came on,
the club erupted into a Hollywood musical.

It was all in my imagination,
mused Blaze in his verses,

that there and then,
all the women
and all the men
in the common areas, and

all the couples from behind the veil, and
the Seductive Queen of Midnight Hair,
who approached me on center stage,

and Sergio to the side, his eyes aglow
with evil, and the security guards and
three waitresses, the resentful cashier,

the tall African Americans, and
the Chinese, Japanese, Philippinos,
the Iranians, Saudis, Ugandans,

everyone was a dancer and singer in the
world chorus, rocking shimmying singing,

Gringo Star in the lead with trimmed white
beard and hat and cane put to good use,

O my my!
O my my!
Can you boogie!
Can you slide!

O my my!
O my my!
Can you boogie!
Can you fly!

Then, just as suddenly as the musical
had begun, the club returned to normal.

New couples formed, new ping-pong
and pool players attracted the crowd.

The security guards and waitresses
returned to their usual omnipresence.

XIV

Blaze mused, sitting on a bench
with his tea, So different are we,
some of us more so than others.

Salvador Sanchez defeated poverty,
winning his title in Las Vegas, and later
stopping Wilfredo Gomez, though the
latter fought valiantly with a closed eye.

Sanchez grew careless and was
killed in one of his sports cars.

The winners grow content,
the compulsive have cancer,
the controlling are autistic,

the extremists dyslexic, the
loners alcoholics or food
or drug or emotion addicts.

The differences are always
both mental and physical.

Isaiah Brown is a fundamentalist
and a sectarian, avoiding dialogue.

Having known him for years,
Blaze had his suspicions.

The narrow groove in which
he thinks must sustain him.

He does not read about world affairs.
He buys gifts for his daughter made
of elephant tusks and rhino horns.

Blaze had long suspected
that Isaiah was dyslexic.

Blaze Pascal told no one
about Club Zero,
not of his doings,
not of his thoughts.

XV

Still sitting on the bench under the Gary Cooper
portrait, Blaze continued his rambling thoughts,
and wondered if he could set them down in verse.

There is not much we can
do to change our dispositions
or combat their associated
diseases and disorders if any.

Learn to accept ourselves
for who we are, and
learn to manage ourselves.

Keep it quiet on the western front.
Keep it simple on the western front.

Don't spend money on sports cars.
Give up the Polaris three-wheeled
motor bicycle and the antique MG
you've coveted for many years.

Don't wait till the wee small hours
of the morning burning with envy.

Walk out while you can.
Protect your freedom
while you still can,
as Grablowski said.

One step backward taken
might save your world too.

Don't keep watching the movable
screens that veil the dancers.

Walk away! Detach yourself!
The drumbeat of the Hebrew,
Christian, Buddhist, Persian,

and Indian sutras and verses
pounded within Blaze P and
drowned out the rock and roll.

Sudden cries came from the
players of ping-pong and pool.

Hearing Angel Baby he became
a mystic, larger than life, and

vainly reached for love
among the stars and
inside the Green Door.

Driving home through the
Bora Bora wilderness of
urban sprawl, beauty was
the moon moving through
shining streaking clouds.

XVI

Blaze Pascal listened for the word
when he heard the wind in the pines,
and when he heard running water.

Be guided by the moon in the river,
said the voice of the Tahquamenon
in the Hiawatha National Forest,

on the trail at night between
the Upper and Lower Falls.

The word came to him from the
Jordan at the cliffs of Qumran,
saying, Call the city to the river,

this river in the desert wilderness,
for healing, grace, and guidance.
The city is insufficient unto itself.

He would sit on Sunday
afternoons on the big
boulders at Thunder
Rock, dangerous in
wind and rain, and the

cliffs near Hunter Beach,
in Acadia National Park,
listening to the power
of the waves crashing
against the rocky shore.

He was lonely on the rocks,
insufficient unto himself.

He looked for lovers along the
cliffs and boulders at the beach,
in the picnic areas, among the
shrub and aspen briar patches

and granite outcroppings along
the mountain trails, and in the
woods around Jordan Pond,
taking pleasure in their bliss,

oblivious of how much he was to learn
about himself and human relationships at
the little church on the river in Maine,

the church of Jerusha Bethelheim, who
fed finches with her hand in the winter,

the church of Olivia Shattuck, who said
that homosexuals hide behind the law,

and he had said that that's what the law is
for, to protect their rights, isn't it? She
had looked at him in such a goofy way.

The soil and the rocks and the
gushing streams spoke to him.
He stored them in his heart.

He kept some smooth pebbles from a beach on his table
for years, and had them returned to the very same beach.

They would speak to him, and
gradually he grew to understand,
but not without hanging his head
over and hearing the wind blow.

He promised that he would return
them exactly where he found them.

XVII

Blaze P was grateful now in the Ground of Being,
where he found friends and life in community, and
the time to write his contemplative poetic lines,

though as he grew older, he had less time to
visit the desert, the mountains, and the sea.

He sought his redemption no longer
in the mythology of the mortal mind,
and he was conflicted about religion.

Zen was popular here, as was
the morass of old metaphysics.

He avoided intolerance, which was rife,
and shunned moralism, which was common.

One condemned a book at the table, though
it was written by a widely acclaimed author,

another censured a movie of suspense,
and still another a lush movie of romance.

Even the brightest,
thinking they were
wise, were worlded.

The religion was worlded,
the theology was worlded.

Comic drifters had strayed in and out of
the mist of his life since Craig Sudsbury,
speeding around in his green 1953 MG
when they were together finishing college,

and Duke Herzegovina with his
London Fog and private eye hat.

Duke had had a pointed nose, wore
dark-rimmed glasses, and led him
around to parties, introduced him to
girls, showed him how to be cool.

Now here came Pushpa Mesmerano with her mat,
her head held high and floating in the air, telling him
about the Chinese soloist in Disney Hall yesterday.

She spread her arms to express
her appreciation of the pianist.
Then she hurried away to yoga.

She was an individualist.
Her hair was wild. She did
what she pleased. No one
pressed her for information.

XVIII

Blaze Pascal, philosopher,
mystic, suspicious of belief
systems, which foster, he said,

the fragmentation and identity
alluded to by the man from
Geneva, still searching for a
common faith, now grew

aware of his own Platonic
mysticism, a mysticism
of being itself, which is
identical with the good.

The good is known to us by its forms
or abstract ideas, truth, beauty, justice,
courage, love, compassion, freedom,

humility, restraint, and understanding,
all conceptual theoretical entities, but

it is these we seek to perceive
and seek to practice in
the kingdom of deprived souls.

We perceive and practice them
he knew, only by our reaching

upward and downward,
outward and inward.

Their instances and manifestations
are always only partial, and
regrettably fall short of perfection.

In our reach we know, wrote Blaze, that
we carry the treasure in earthen vessels,

and that our reaching itself
is enabled in part by grace.

We know too that our pursuit of
truth, beauty, and the forms of goodness
faces the ridicule and persecution
of the darkness of the worlded mind.

Mashal Khan was a Pakistani university student
recently beaten and killed by a mob for being anti-
Islamic. He was a humanist and Marxist promoting
women's rights, racial justice, and freedom for all.

The beating and killing of
this enlightened soul
saddened Blaze P deeply.

Fundamentalism is
rife all over the world.
It is sad but true.

The extremist mind is
drawing the world,
drawing it unto itself.

Those who seek truth and justice face
the narrow-mindedness of the world,

like Socrates and Jesus,
Boethius and Gandhi,
and Martin Luther King Jr.

Missing in the conversation is
the light of literature, science, and
the atmosphere of philosophy.

This is the contemporary spiritual quandary.

Such were the thoughts of Blaze Pascal,
as he sat in one of the academic libraries
in the town-gown city of trees and Ph.Ds.

XIX

Blaze Pascal continued
his verses with diligence.
He sought energy, rhythm,
keeping the youth in mind.

His pile of scratch paper
grew higher and higher.

Quandary, quandary.
Contemporary quandary.

Practice prudence, self-control.
Use restraint, protect the soul.

Beware of the traps
that bedevil the mind.
Distraction ensnares
and pride enslaves.

Know your limitations.

Resist the current,
the growing dark.
Spread the light,
share the spark.

Protect the sources of light.

The extremists burned
down Laubach Hall and
the school in Mindanao.

They burned down Frank C. Laubach Hall!
They burned down Frank C. Laubach Hall!

Take time to be quiet.
Reach for the truth,
reach for beauty,

downward, upward,
inward and outward.

Then will ideas bloom,
like deep red poppies,

and knowledge be fragrant,
like the bank of elyssium
behind the new coffee and
tea shop in the village,

and the light and love shine
of literature and philosophy.

The word upon the wind and
the waters is what rises in
the soul when one hears them.

It is the word of being itself,
and it is this that unworlds me.

Look not for success to the
powers and principalities,
where moth and rust corrupt
and time itself is a thief.

If thought is confined to a narrow
scheme, let your discontent be known.

Insist that the frame of reference
be the infinitely expanding horizon.

Moth and rust cannot corrupt,
and time itself cannot steal
the courage of being
in the face of nonbeing.

They cannot steal
poverty of spirit,
radical humility,

the practice of restraint,
reverence for life,
depth of thought,
the respect for beauty.

XX

Essence and existence
take turns in being prior,
though some say flatly
existence is prior, and
some that essence is prior.

And note the dialectical relation
between universals and particulars.

A universal points to its particulars,
and particulars lead to their universal.

Knowledge is an Olympic gold medal in this town,
though it is only one side of our world experience.

Attend to the full robe of many tones,
textures, and colors, not the fragment.

Justice is the color of surfers
appearing and disappearing
on the horizon of the sea,

like the happy see-saw of
essence and existence,
universal and particular.

Freedom is Uzma wading beaming screaming,

her first time in the sea, Sharif loving the carnival,
the blissful shouts of children above the waves.

Beauty is a deodar on a mountain ridge, a
forest below of rhododendrons in the mist,

and the undersides of ferns.
Rare ferns with difficult names,
Adiantum capillus veneris,
Athyrium pectinatum,
Polypodium microhiza.

It was the beauty of the forest
and its ferns and its flowers and
its wild animals that made us
love Dr. Perkins and his classes.

Courage is the color of marigolds, their
garlands for weddings, for Christmas,
petal decorations over food for the gods.

Love is a brilliant sunset,
though it comes and goes,

and some stand alone
among pines and palms,
watching the birds come home
and the sun sink into the sea.

These together are the worship
the magi know they must seek, to
which the star necessarily leads.

These they must take home,
one whole cloth,
for the generations to come.

They interpenetrate, they
invoke, one another, like
chords in a composition.

XXI

The verses of Blaze Pascal
harkened back to his past.

My train was stopped in the night
at the small station of Kurukshetra.

Here under the full moon was the site
of the Bhagavad Gita's mythic battle
and the teaching of the embodied soul.

Here too was the hanging
of Gandhi's assassin,
Godse the fundamentalist,

where the gods of
truth mocked him.

A solitary vendor went by,
chanting garm chai, garm chai,
dark against the moon.

Word, wisdom, logos, truth,
and all the big ideas of the
good, have been the courage
and consolation of my years.

Once I covered the waterfront, watching the sea.
Watching for no one, no one was coming for me.

Then I learned the dialogue of the
Golden Bridge of Transcendence
and the Greyhound bus schedule.

The bus took me across the bridge
from the city set on a hill to
freedom in the city by the bay, and

back across to the freedom
of the city set on a hill.

Across the bridge on both sides was truth.
On the one side was the truth of Karl Barth,
who said No to the nineteenth century liberals,

finding them swallowed up
by Babylon, which extended
as far as the eye could see,

shaken like a reed
by the currents of
the modern world.

On the other was the truth of Market Street,
where I saw Love Is a Many-Splendored Thing
and Marlon Brando in The Young Lions.

Across the bridge on both sides was love.
On the one side were my seminary friends
in my classes, my dorm, the dining hall,
and Taylor, the girl I wouldn't romance.

On the other the girls on the stages of burlesque
and screens of movie theaters and adult parlors.

On both sides of the bridge was music,
Be Thou My Vision on the one,
In the Still of the Night on the other,
though I never did get to the hungry i.

The foghorns were for me the blues,
and there was always the jukebox,

the jukebox,
the jukebox,
the jukebox,

for Blueberry Hill and Stand by Me
and Sinatra's Tell Her You Love Her.

On both sides was confinement.
They became an Alcatraz, and
the bridge meant transcendence,
the passage over swift currents.

The young man told no one
of his night visits to the city.

No, even then, he was
afraid of narrow minds.

He wrote a confession later, but
as he matured into adulthood,
he knew his letter to be a mistake.

XXII

Sitting in Platonic Coffee
at University and Church,
with students and young
families with children,

and retirees and the very
old whirling around him,
Blaze P put this down.

At Point Conception the ground is soft and
crunchy, with its gold dust and tiny pale green
and red berries of cedar and mesquite and pine.

The fog, the wind,
the strand, and the
blue of sea and sky
on a clear day,

are elements so simple, some of them, that
their essences are the elements themselves,

not abstract ideas or forms,
universals or postulations.

Air, water, red, and blue,
they have no definition
to grasp with the intellect.

We cannot explain, only point to,
what we breathe, drink, perceive.

If a man asks for a definition of water, you must
take him to the stream and say, This, this is water.

The universe is alive!
Even the abstractions
are perceptively active
through their instances.

Beauty is a Thou at
Point Conception.

The interaction is of love,
I and Thou, between an
old man and the ground.

I sit and stare at the sea.
Slowly I step in and the
waves splash against me.

The dynamic is love,
I and Thou, between
the old man and the sea.

Ideas arise as
ideas-of,

ideas of how,
ideas of when,
ideas of where.

They occur in the heat of situations,
though they may create situations.

The idea of justice arises in
the course of negotiations,
though it may come first
and create the negotiations.

The idea of secular arises in
the course of investigations,
though it may come first
and create the investigations.

They inform one another,
ideas and situations.
They concur and confirm,
they rebuke and revise.

XXIII

Blaze Pascal's verses at
Platonic Coffee continued.

The voice of a ten-year-old girl in
Tahrir Square glued me to the radio.

Listen, Mr. President,
we're speaking to you!

Ten thousand repeated
the lines each time.

Your people are dead!
They live in garbage on the street!
Ten thousand repeated the words.

The essence of freedom,
through its individual chants,
was actualized on the streets.

Yesterday I rang two sounds,
a red bell on blue stained glass,
in the dining hall for grace.

In between I mentioned
love for all suffering beings,
the yoga of deep thought,

the courage of being in
the face of nonbeing.

To the four corners the
two sounds rang and
cast their insinuations.

And the abstract forms
love, thought, and courage
resounded in the world

XXIV

Hold me close at the
Khyber Pass between
world and ground of being.

Kiss me my love
at the border between
sacred and profane.

Stand by me in
the drone-zone between
fact and form.

From the tribal region of Pakistan,
the mountain land of the Pathans,

come Sharif, the new seminary student,
speaker of several languages, his wife
Uzma, and their one-year-old Princess,
with whom I play Red Rubber Ball.

Sharif is intelligent, hard-working.
He keeps track, knows we are turning
south, changing freeways, passing the
Newport Beach city limit sign.

He asks of the meaning of liberal and exegesis.
He keeps in good graces with his professors.

With his wife too. She too is bright, asks at
their table over rice and dal about fatalism.

She spends a good deal of time
in children's departments, sifting
rapid-fire through the racks. They
ask me to take them shopping.

Princess resembles her mother, and a
special bonding exists between them.
It will be her second birthday soon.

They are puristic about their foods,
their Bollywood music, their movies,
their literalism in matters of religion.

Not fruits and veggies as
much as meat and milk.

Not the stars at Griffith Park, but
photos to send back home of
the Hollywood sign behind them.

Silently she showed me the marks on her arms
from the bombing of their church in Peshawar.
We were sitting in the Brahmaputra on Gower.

They lost their two older boys.

He lost his mother and father.

Once the Frontier Mail would stop at my
home town on its return from Peshawar
on its way to Delhi and far beyond.

The monster engine would come around the bend
and the buzzing platform flashed red with coolies.

Fear of the hissing steam and screaming whistle
made the ten-year-old shut his ears and his eyes.

My family came at Christmas
from Lahore and Rawalpindi,
from Amritsar and Delhi, for
my grandfather's long prayers,

blessing everyone by name
in the crowded dining room.

Shattered some were as families,
yet they wore their finest clothes.

Still they came after the Partition,
after the fragmentation and identity,
crossing the mighty, muddy Sutlej.

Uncle Priti was the only one absent from
among my father's sisters and brothers,
though his wife and children were there.
He was bright, funny, scrappy, ambitious.

He had disappeared, gone
some said to Great Britain.

Some said he had become rich
dealing in underground jewels or
arms deals with the Arab states.

I saw him once in his new car and
smelled the leather, inspected the
dashboard and hollows of the seats.
It was shortly after the Partition.

XXV

Blaze Pascal's verses labored on
for depth, elegance, and expansion
in philosophy, religion, literature,

inspired by April is
the cruelest month,

in debt to Socrates,
Schliermacher,
Boethius, Tillich,

to Alonzo Church, who was influenced by
Gottlob Frege, and became himself a Platonist:

If they could be Platonists,
why couldn't Blaze himself?

Church's elegance in Chapter Zero and
the formal systems knew no bounds.
Blaze had never read anyone like him.

He admired the simplicity of
the self-distributive law, the law
of affirming the consequent,
and the law of double negation,

and the power these three axioms had to
generate the whole propositional system.

Blaze worked at the proofs all the time
and everywhere, taking his scratchings

with him to the bank, the cafe, the library,
just like he took his verse scratchings now.

Alonzo Church, with a mind of
pure reason and wildly creative
soul, taught the young man how
to think, and he emerged truly

as Blaze Pascal, gaining
confidence in himself as
a philosopher advancing
in the Platonic process.

That he could grasp the material
and hear the flow of the music that
sounded so right page by page,
this changed him fundamentally.

The nominalistic writings of Willard Van Orman Quine, Nelson
Goodman, and Morton White now sounded off-key to his ears.

White's critiques of Niebuhr on inevitability and Emerson
on the oracles of the heart always did sound wrong anyway.

Blaze grew fat with new possible worlds within, and
his future bloomed with new possible worlds without,

though he would soon know
the human imperfections
of the academic community,

and grow to know
his own limitations.

The world would hardly be elegant,
like Chapter Zero, or behave like a
formal system as described there.

To Marlon Brando
in Viva Zapata and
The Young Lions,
Blaze was grateful,

as he was to the Pynchon sites on the web.
He followed the links wherever they went,

to the Doc Portello narrative in the movie
about the beach town and its bums,
to all the reviews and the featured articles.

To the James Joyce sites too,
the graphics and the excerpts.

And the music of
Rhapsody in Blue,
Abbey Road, and
Barber's Adagio,

he said, expressed
just the right tones,

deep and sad, and were
yet energetic, rhythmic,

the tones and rhythms for which he listened
on the radio, and which eluded him
when he sought to express them in his writing.

XXVI

Blaze Pascal took his turn
and spoke the word, and

then said philosophical
things, Freedom itself,
as he broke the bread,

Love itself, as he
poured the cup.

The point of word is liberation,
the point of sacrament is love.

The pulpit alone, or
the table alone, is
not the whole cloth.

This is the noble truth
of freedom and love.

There must be freedom in
love and love in freedom.

Freedom without love turns violent,
love without freedom is oppressive.

Slight frame, come, receive your strength!
Mean spirit, come, here is your song!
Wavering soul, come, claim your voice!

Some looked puzzled.
Is this not a bit pagan?

Blaze then slipped into self-doubt
about his example and leadership,

and finding himself conflicted
about the church community, its

liturgy, its music, its sermons,
its prayers, and its piety, he
began to move toward the fringe,

serving only as greeter at the door,
convening a theological group, but

still uncertain within himself about the church's
ability to elevate the soul toward enlightenment,
to a critical hermeneutic receptive of philosophy.

But was it not possibly the
only place to go for a seeker
on the streets of loneliness,
on the streets of anxiety?

The streets without comfort,
without love or assurance.

Where could an average seeker go
for guidance, strength, and refuge?

There were times when Blaze lingered outside
the door to hear the singing of the first hymn.

Tears welled up within him at
the singing of All Glory, Laud,
and Honor on Palm Sunday.

He left during the first verse.

His friends said they missed him, and
asked why he doesn't worship with them.

He said that he migrates now
between sacred and secular,
between solitude and community,

between the mountains and the sea,
between the city and the wilderness.

In this is my enlightenment,
and in this my consolation.

XXVII

Whose piano do I hear,
playing so softly?
Whose singing do I hear,
so strong, so deep?

The piano is the waves
lapping against the shore.
The singing is the wind
in the pines and cedars.

The music is the music of the
soul, of the whole being, the
heart, the senses, the intellect.

Blaze Pascal, standing
at Point Conception,
knew the joy and strength,

of the ones who linger on the
big rock overlooking the sea,

and walk upon the crunchy ground of
the pine and the mesquite, their
leaves of rust and red and green berries.

Just yesterday at lunch he had watched
two people talk to each other hysterically
about something coming right up. They
were out of breath, breathing so rapidly.

Then came another friend to talk
to a woman urgently and hastily,
looking into her eyes earnestly.

Will you be there?
Blaze read his lips.

And Blaze met another man along his walk.
He was carrying a bag and seemed in a rush.

Where are you going, my friend? asked Blaze.
The man said, pointing, They're having a week
of prayer down there, which I've been attending

At Point Conception healing
and inner strength come, not in
a rush, but as you hear the

waves splash and the wind
blow and shape you as surely
as the water carves the shore
and the wind curves the pines.

Blaze heard the music of big truth,
compelling and consequential,
the knowledge of good and evil,
the knowledge of right and wrong.

It was the music of his youth.
He had fled to the rhododendron
tree to eat his parcel of sweets,
its bark the color of clay, like

the ground itself, its flower
casting a red glow upon the slope.
That tree was with him now.

He lingered too at the pine-lit
place with the abandoned cabin.

He could look across the valley
to the schools on the other side.
That place that was with him now.

Consoled he has been by cottonwoods
at the wide Missouri and the Great
Plains of the prairie and the buffalo,

by hemlocks in the northeast, and
the great cedars in the northwest.
The past is never just the past.

Blaze hears music
at Point Conception
of Satyagraha, freedom,
the love for all beings.

Kenneth D. Stephens

Thus his mysticism grows,
and he is not alone. White

flags of aspiration flutter
in the Himalayan breeze.

People seek and hear the good
on every side of the mountain:

Healing for the nations
in the leaves of the trees
at the river that flows
from the eternal snows.

Freedom in the desert
and the purple sage
and the cactus blue.

The voice says,
Come away,
come away.

Come away from
the fragmentation
and the identity.

What rises in
the bubbles
at the pond

and widens in
the circles
is compassion.

What is heard
in the buzz
of the bees

and known
in the flight
of the dragons

is the serenity
that feeds the
deprived mind.

XXVIII

Beyond the little village
in White Rock Ravine,

travelers walk warily
in sage and cactus,

home of rattlesnakes,
haunt of cougars. Here

the hawk dives,
the raven dodges.

Eagles circle, and
blackness penetrates
the blue from beyond.

Bluejays call out to opposing slopes.

Hikers stoop at rivulets to
view their souls in pools.

Some ask for the road that leads
to the north of Vulture Mountain,
to the river which has no name,

where the mystery prophet lives
who calls to the city to come,
but no one knows of such a road.

The chaparral thins
at the higher elevations
of Vulture Mountain,

yielding first to pines, then to
sculpted low-growing shrubs and
jagged trees with naked limbs.

They who venture higher
to Contemplation Ridge
practice the goodness of

unlearning, criticism, and
radical spiritual humility.

They know their limitations, which
is the smallness of their knowledge.

They know only the immediate road:
They judge what's coming down ahead.

The Ridge can be narrow, the
winds excessive from both sides.
Only one may cross at a time.

The Jew may not debar the Arab,
the Arab may not despise the Jew.

The American may not detain or deport the immigrant.

The Christian may not decry the Muslim,
the Muslim may not deprive the Christian.

XXIX

The verses of Blaze Pascal, being
written currently in a seminar room,
looking up at Mount Contemplation,
at the theological seminary library,

grew ever more mindful of
tone and rhythm,
style and frame of reference.

I met Duke on the road in
my college days, they said.

The Duke, with pointed features,
nerdy glasses, and wiry figure:

He hinted at all the
places he had been.

The Duke, with London Fog
and suave way with words:

He hinted at all the
things he had seen.

His world was prosperous,
and he was coddled in it.

Kenneth D. Stephens

At a folk-rock event the warm
glow of the polished floor
on and around the stage
centered the sweeping surfer blue.

Sixty or seventy delirious
students filled the space.

The songs were sad-happy, poignant,
with lyrics of love lost and love found
and Who Knows Where Time Goes?

The Duke vanished into the crowd.
An intoxicated youth rubbed against
another, insinuating the actual thing.

I asked some who stood beside me
about the direction of their studies,
but it was loud talk everywhere,

though these same elite students would
attend the Vietnam War debates and
join the civil rights and peace sit-ins,
stand-ups, drop-outs, and marches.

The Pope too resides in luxuriance,
though he himself is a humble man.

And a valiant man to
write his Laudato Si.

It sways believers
in some respects in
the right direction.

He can hardly know that he looks at
life through the rose-colored glasses
of wealth and power, and of a colossal
theology inherited from an ancient past.

He can hardly see how his Encyclical
cannot understand the foundations of
the modern spiritual quandary, the

fragmentation itself, the identity itself,
and the absence of Socratic dialogue.

And not a word about the status of women!
Not a word about human overpopulation,
the root cause of the shrinking wilderness,

the clear-cutting of the forests, the draining
of the coast lands and deltas, the slums of
Mumbai, New Delhi, Calcutta, and Mexico
City, the general degradation of human life!

To renounce the palaces
of power and prosperity,
both material and spiritual,
and practice the Beatitudes,

becoming makers of peace,
poor in spirit, pure in heart,

scaling the steeps of
unlearning, climbing
the crags of criticism,
literature, philosophy,

such disciplines are necessary for the soul,
and such is the ultimate landscape of spirit.

Thus the perishable puts
on imperishability, the
mortal immortality, and
death has no dominion.

And yes, dead ones naked,
they are one with the man in
the moon and the west wind.

XXX

On the road below of
dust and crumbling rock,

we grieve our errors and
reappraise our situations,

given the present turmoil
of terror and surveillance,
fragmentation and identity.

Again we reminisce of
the people and places,

those that received us,
those that refused us,
those that opened
our inward eyes.

I saw them through the pines,
walking on the rickshaw road.

We were sixteen then, she and I,
and no longer children playing
hopscotch in the yard that looked
down upon the rocks of nonbeing.

She was the first I loved, when
love became the terrible secret
I did not know or understand,
much less embrace without fear.

Though she is dead, she is alive.
I saw her again through the pines.

XXXI

Blaze, the straggling soul, on the
road of dust and crumbling rock,
still slowly learning, floundering,

sought in clubs and dialogue circles,
in cafes, cafeterias, and classrooms,

and the solitude of sea and sage,
mesquite and the mean streets,
mountain rock and music theory,

a deeper way of being in the world,
and with it a deeper understanding.

The principle that sacred listening
is prior to all inquiry, and what is
heard is prior to factual knowledge,

this teaching of the Vedas, and
Dharmic religion in general,
came newly to him as a practice.

And poverty of spirit, as
taught in the Beatitudes, was
the answer he was given,

this radically simple answer to
the modern spiritual quandary.

A man came in with his wife and
declared in Blaze's dialogue session,
Abrahamic monotheism causes wars!

Dr. Graham Dorsey was a thin man
with a long face, a pointed nose,
and white curly hair that fell below
his ears and flew loose in the wind.

Both an activist and a deep thinker,
he was a knowledgeable man,
with an American Friends Service
Committee background. He had
risked all by making boycott and

disinvestment decisions in a
corporate, capitalistic world,
as president of universities
and theological seminaries.

In his retirement he took foreign visitors,
lately from Mozambique and South Africa,

to the Watts Riots sites, Disney Hall, and
the Griffith Observatory in the magical city
of music, movie stars, and mean streets.

His wife Isabelle went with him.
She went everywhere with him.
She walked slowly with a cane,
and he walked slowly beside her.

She was diminutive and wrinkled,
but she was pretty in her old age.
She had retired after thirty years
of chaplaincy in a major university

working with Catholic, Jewish, Islamic, Presbyterian,
Lutheran, United Methodist, and other Protestant clergy.

A door swung open for Blaze
Pascal: He took courage from

Graham's declaration on
Abrahamic monotheism,

and wondered if Graham
was influenced by Isabelle
in theological matters,

the way he always leaned and
listened closely to her at table.

Blaze was happy that he heard Graham that day, and
he grew grateful for their presence there at Ground.

Kenneth D. Stephens

XXXII

And Blaze Pascal wrote this
looking out to the west after
sunset at the bright quarter moon

and the luminous Evening Star
through the palms and the pines:

Hear my song
Desert Moon:

Silver light on
sand and stone,

Dharmic emptiness
and dry bones. A

whole valley
of dry bones.

Primitive shapes,
desolate spaces.

The law of double negation
is part of the foundation.

The coyote howls,
the jaguar prowls.

Human shadows
seeking sanctuary
move northward.

I left everything behind
except the bare necessities.

All my things were
in my small Toyota,

my radio and CD player with speakers,
clothes, cooking materials, my papers
and reference books, not more than ten.

Where is your U-Haul?
Where is your U-Haul?
they asked when I arrived.

Come down, people,
join us in the streets!

The gods of identity,
NULL AND VOID!

The gods of fragmentation,
NULL AND VOID!

Hold your head high!
Soon you will be free!

XXXIII

Blaze went inside his cottage
and continued his verses:

Before I sold my cabin,
two fawns pranced outside,
and the mystic voice asked,

Where are the gray wolf and the spotted owl?
Where are the bumblebee and the wild fowl?

Short was the day.
The sun hastened
upon the sky's curve.

The forest withdrew
for its tenebrae.

Was it not for this
I gave all I had
to buy the land and
build the cabin,

to keep the fire burning,
fetch the pale of water,
to cook the dal and rice,

to make my way
through the woods
to the river?

Was it not for this,
to be alone in the
face of nonbeing?

Yet I fled from fear.

The neighbors were hostile to me
from the beginning, when I bought

the lot and built my fire in the
light of the firmament of stars.

One evening my date was Marlene,
who had striking European features.

Her curls, dimples, and big brown eyes
might have driven the man insane, just
as they did me and all the other men.

A professional cellist who played in a
well-known modern music ensemble,

she was uncomfortable and hated the
hike through the underbrush, over the logs,
along the craggy banks of the river.

I loved Marlene, but she could perceive
that I didn't have the right future for her.

And when we found that my old manual
drip-style coffee pot and the cups that
matched were no longer at the campsite,
she was frightened and wanted to leave.

We both knew who stole them: We had
seen the man through the evergreens.

Another man spoke rudely to me from his
vehicle as I filled my pale from the spring.

I had no fear when
I had come out to look
at the property and

watch the moon move
through the forest

and up to the ridge
where the sun set,

and the shooting stars
streak through the sky,
ignoring the boundaries
of galaxies and nebulae,

keeping their knowledge to themselves,
where they come from, where they go,
what they've seen, what they've heard.

It was racist tabloid minds
that made me wary later
of such a remote location
for my place of solitude.

XXXIV

No, the shooting stars
will not stop to
share their knowledge
or their love.

We are left
to speculate
and create,

to still watch,
to still listen,

to peruse the verses
of old souls and
attend to the mantras
of ancient temples.

As the cucumber matures
and is freed from the vine,

so liberate us from
attachment and death.

The chants return
to the same refrain,

Sweet gladness and
strength for the soul are
the signs we're given.

So much we see,
so little we seize.

So much we hear,
so little we heed.

XXXV

Seized by beauty
when it appears,
we shall dance
if only we ask.

Nothing stops old man Blaze,
still watching for such appearances
and listening for such sounds.

He crosses the widening eyes of
the nineteen other men wavering.

They note his walk, they
look him up and down,
they want to know who
he is and what he does.

What makes him so bold,
to pick out Genevieve,
the stand-out starlet of

the Creative City,
and hold her hand
as they go to dance?

The cheetah features he
sees are only surface.
He withholds judgment.

The first words are spoken,
and he is drawn into a red
zone, the zone of love, in the

nocturnal glow on the dancing
side of the veil of ignorance.

Articulate, and with nothing to
hide, she tells him her situation,

her annoyances with the recent man,
who came for her to the Abyss and
had to be forced out by a guard, the
Goldfinger strongman up in the front,

her waffling over the current man,
who she lives with now and who
drives her here, stays in the city,
and then comes to take her home.

She is explicit about her autism and
knowledgeable about what it means.

Rocky shore,
warped pine,
of jagged love.

Linear mind,
angular meaning,
of this impossible other.

She is in control,
yet she is sirenic,

she is love the stranger,
gesturing him on, when
there is no visible danger.

Desire grows,
truth now flows,

a paper boat in Angel River,
which flows from the San
Gabriels to San Pedro Bay
under the brazen towers,

under the One-Ten, the Five, the One-O-One,
under Wilshire, Figueroa, and Union Station,

under City Hall and Disney Hall
and the bridges and flyways of

a civilization unknowing, a
megalopolis interchanging.

XXXVI

Blaze Pascal will be back
again and again
to seek out Genevieve.

His eyes will pierce
the veil of ignorance,

the silken hangings,
the tropical plants, that
hide the dancing couples.

There will be others
who she will draw,
rich men, who will

spend more time with her
and tip her well in the zone.

Tiptoe he will find in
the moving shadows
the hair that flairs
and is made of gold.

But he will be on
this side of the veil.

XXXVII

The next time Blaze
learned more of autism,

how it stands stiff
in the arms of love.

It cannot reach below,
it cannot plumb the
depth of the passion.

The bulbs flash red and blue, legs
kick forward, backward, sideways.

Shoes come off, shirts flair,
silky fabrics fly in the air.

The passing show, a powerful light,
helps you make it through the night,

but gives no mental benefaction,
and no real physical satisfaction.

One-night love will not come true
in a metro hotel on Santa Monica or
a desert motel on Route Sixty-Six.

Even now around you rise the
towers with a thousand eyes.

You were just one of the lonely men,
just one fevered link in the ontic chain,

searching anonymously for love in the
city of mean streets and movie stars.

Improbable the solidarity,
standing shoulder to shoulder

with businessmen and lawyers, doctors and bankers,
foreign corporate officials and blue collar workers.

No more the moon. The
foggy overhang is all in all

in the parking lot
under the Kienholz '36.

You cannot make out
the back seat figures
in the wee small hour,

but you see them
in your mystic mind,
with your private eye,
as you drive home.

XXXVIII

Though Blaze tells no one of
his night visits to the big city,
he does write his verses to
do what shooting stars don't,

namely leave behind his
secret knowledge in his
philosophical manuscript.

He talks to no one about his private life.
No one needs to know about what was
The Lonely Dragon in the old days,

before they changed the name to The
Abyss, because it sounds contemporary,

or about the other clubs he visited long
ago, before they were closed, or the
new clubs he visits quite regularly now.

I look over Jordan,
and what do I see?

Satyagraha, the
creative good,
watching over me,

life, love, and freedom,
truth, justice, beauty,
and the courage to be.

On this side of Jordan I
ask the question of trust.

And a voice cries,
All flesh is grass.

Protect your freedom, you must.
Protect the beauty, you must.

Yes, I say, all flesh is grass,
and few know their limits.

I meet addicts everywhere.
Their knowledge is painful
of things they cannot attain.

No one understands how
it weighs upon their soul.

They will seek a way,
all flesh seeks a way,
to keep the pain at bay.

They will not be told
their condition to behold.

Tony was a starving actor,
his behavior idiosyncratic,
soon it looked bizarre.

When I came to know
him, I confronted him.
He took his revenge.

Last night I had a dream.
I was with Marlene, or
someone like Marlene,
at a social gathering.

I saw a man visit with with her.
He was bigger and taller than I.

Truly my loves have been
nebulous, dark, and deep, and
the dream was agony for me.

The Ground of Being has
been a good place for me.

I have time to write, and
I have made good friends.

Yet many cannot fathom a life
devoid of a religious framework.

Many are sexually pure,
who have linear minds
and a worlded theology.

Though they speak in the
tongues of mortals and angels,
they resist the influence of
literature and philosophy.

The mythic narrative clouds and
clutters the mind of pious souls.

XXXIX

All flesh is grass.
The verses of life and death
are blowing in the breeze.

The leaves of the trees
are falling on the pavement.

Falling and running,
running upon falling.

The radio is playing
a popular song sung
by Lata Mandeshkar,

The magical night has passed away.
I have no idea when you will come.

It is evening, and Raj and Bhagavant are
sitting outside on a bed with their parents,

the goat beside them,
a well just beyond, and
a partially desolate field
where some fly kites.

Raj is my age and is like his father,
literal, with only one window open,
always mixing grain, carrying manure.

The father is stern, a hard
worker at the hospital.

Bhagavant is plump and playful, his
face fair and smooth like his mother's,

their line going back perhaps to
Greek, Turk, and Persian
invasions through the Khyber Pass.

He is the younger brother, and
he has many windows open.

The mother is quiet,
stays at home, and
is very friendly to us.

It is too late to play, they say. We are
fixed on our slates with arithmetic. The
school master is strict and demanding.

Perhaps tomorrow we can walk
in the moonlight and pull turnips
when the gardener is asleep. The
evening has stolen by like a thief.

XL

Blaze Pascal wrote it all down,
how Violence persists on both
sides, the crimes of the cartels, the
deportation of the undocumented.

Asylum pleas are mostly denied,
based on government policy, not
adjudicated on individual merit.

Some dare practice kindness
in the face of the madness.

They open their churches
for seekers of sanctuary.

They stand at stations on
the journey in the desert
for those fleeing the terror.

Archbishop Oscar Romero spoke out
for the peasants on the radio.
Everyone urban and rural listened.

But March is the cruelest month.

One sermon called the soldiers to
cease the killing and repression.

He was assassinated the next day on March 23,
serving communion in a San Salvador hospital.

The death squad gunman took
aim with his rifle, fired, and saw
the blood pour out from his victim
and onto the elements on the altar.

This is my blood
poured out for you.
Do this....

The shot was heard around the world.
The death of this incarnation of word
will be remembered. It will never die.

They killed his body
but not his soul, the
light he exemplified.

It will sadden the hearts of all
whose hearts are magnanimous.

XLI

A Salvadoran nun just died
in Angel City of her injuries.

A former nun, back from Guatemala,
walks her dog at the Ground of Being.

This evening as we walk
she says there is no road.
The road is the way we go.

She remembers what happened
there in the middle of the night.

Open the gate!
Open the gate!
They have killed Father Tulio!

The church went underground then.
She and her convent fled to Chiapas,
suspected all of liberation theology.

The Mayan Indians followed
with everything they had.
Accused of communism, they
fled when there was no moon.

But I heard their voices
in the light of a big moon.

They burned our villages,
tortured our people,

killed our babies and
hung them in the trees.

They butchered pregnant women
and cut out their fetuses.

They raped our young women
and assassinated our young men
or forced them to join the military.

One mother protested their
taking her teenage son.
She was shot there and then.

In the refugee camp they
slept on tree branches.
There were no toilets,
no medical services.

At her trial my companion,
along with the others, were
shorn of their right in the

glare of the light to tell
the ground they stand on,
why they can do no other.

This was not allowed in
the legalistic court, by
the behavioristic judge.

XLII

Then Blaze Pascal wrote this, I
was standing at Point Conception,

on the rock overhung by
an old short-needle pine,

and what did I see?

I saw the river of being
empty into the sea.

I saw nonviolence
watching over me.

Here the magi
heard the word,

Satyagraha,
the creative good,

from soul and soil
and wind and water
and the drooping mesquite.

The sameness of Atman and Brahman,
the sameness of highest and deepest.

They spoke it out loud in churches, on campuses,
though their voice was muted in the courtrooms,

that healing supplant the fragmentation,
that community replace the identity,

that justice dethrone the oppressors,
and the corrupt be scattered in
the imagination of their hearts.

The rock of deep thought,
the inner rock of deep feeling:

This was the ground they stood on,
and why they could do no other.

Here I met the Archbishop and poet T. S. Eliot,
who spoke of contemplation and renunciation,
known by mystics as the dark night of the soul.

He said to his soul, Be still, and let
the dark come upon you, by
which he meant the same dark night.

Blessed are they who wait without
hope, the hope for worldly things.

Blessed are they who wait without
love, the love of worldly things.

Here I met Rosa Parks, for whom saying
No in Alabama was a mystical act,

and Gandhi, for whom Kurukshetra
was a mystical field, the battleground
of the human soul for truth, not
the place where two armies clashed,

and Henry David Thoreau, who
said, I will go to Walden Pond
to live in radical simplicity
and know the depth of being,

free of hyperactivity, the
uses and abuses of things,
the vulgar aim of prosperity,

and the flattened world
of mainstream opinion.

I will draw from the well of
Walden water and the river that
flows from the eternal snows.

All these persons asked me to
join them on the Loop Trail.

Yes, I said gladly, I will follow
behind you, watching the sea,
listening to the waves
and the wind in the trees.

And Murad Begh and Suniti Pal
were surfing far out in the sea.

They loved each other in college.
I saw them holding hands on the
Number 9 bus, which dropped us
off at the campus in the morning.

But Murad was a Mogul
and Suniti was a Brahmin, and
the system said it was not to be.

Big truths and beautiful things,
they come back to us.

Standing on the waterfront,
they are the figures we see
playing in the sea of light,

the oneness of the human family
beyond the things that divide us,

living in harmony with
wild lands and wild waters,

the love for all beings,
human and nonhuman.

To practice simplicity
is to be a mystic.

To preserve the beauty
of the wilderness
is to be a mystic.

To prevent needless suffering is a
mystical act, and an absolute truth.

To live in solidarity
with suffering beings
is to be a mystic.

Breathing deeply
is a mystical act.

What we breathe is truth.
What we breathe is spirit,
said the Buddhist monk.

What we breathe is
the fragrance of life.

To walk to the post office,
the bank, the public library,
the park, and the cafe, and

to lift your arms and touch
your hands above you ten
times daily, this is mystical.

XLIII

Last night in Club Zero they
played Everybody's Talkin' at Me.

Today I keep hearing the
Midnight Cowboy song.

The singer sings of hearing
only the echoes of his mind,
not the world talking at him.

I saw the movie long ago.
We hear the song play as
the hero is walking away
from the country to the city.

What truth, new and big, awaited him?
What old truth was he running from?
Was there a truth in the journey itself?

Why did I climb Landour Mountain
alone to hear the missionaries sing at
eleven when I was in boarding school?

Why would I go to the city
across the waters of the bay
when I was in seminary?

Why did I cross the big
divide into philosophy?

Why did I seek respite from the city
and build my cabin in the wilderness?

XLIV

At eleven, wrote Blaze, I was
given permission to climb the mountain
to hear the missionaries sing.

Glad songs, they sang, of
freedom above the world,
the abode of homesickness.

At twenty I skipped over the
ocean like a stone to the
freedom of Market Street,

where the sun kept shining
through the pouring rain.

There was truth on both sides of the bridge.

At the seminary it was the truth
of Kierkegaard and Karl Barth.

Theology was a lion,
roaring to be heard,

though Barth himself fled from the
Babylon of wrath and lust and worldly
strife to the Habakkuk mountaintop
fortress of grace, peace, and strength.

On the other side of the
Golden Gate was the city,

and on Fridays and holidays
were the dancing girls
on screen and stage,

the movies at the Fox,
the ice cream stalls,
the adult parlors, and
the jazz at the hungry i.

The Greyhound diner jukeboxes
had the songs I had come to love,
In the Still of the Night, Smoke
Gets in Your Eyes, Stand by Me,

which I played asking for the last of the
apple pie and waiting for the bus at two.

XLV

Truth was rising everywhere,
truth momentous and manifold,
truth principled and profound,
truth essential and existential.

Blaze P fled from belief into doubt,
and from doubt into the
the Platonic elegance of
Gottlob Frege and Alonzo Church.

Big truth was the learning-how,
and a new road came into view.

Its destination was obscure.
It was leading anywhere.
It was leading everywhere.

It was no road at all.
It was wherever he walked,
like the former nun said.

The century drew to a close.
The drivenness of the city
was flattening the human soul.

People were losing control,
the pressures were unrelenting.

The age of compulsion and cancer,
the age of terror and surveillance,
the age of brinksmanship and war,

Blaze could sense it coming.
It was just around the corner.

He searched in the mountains,
he looked in the wilderness,
he went far away to the sea.

He gave all the money he had
to buy the acre in the forest.

He loved the cabin he had built,
the thicker studs of the walls,
everything left uninsulated,

the woodenness of the space,
the cathedral-like ceiling,

the chopping of the wood
for the wood-burning stove,

the scary walk to the river
through the dark woods,

the cooking of the dal and rice,
the baking of the potato in foil,

and the drinking of the water
from the springs of being itself.

It was all about freedom from
stresses internal and external,

the practice of sanity in a world he
believed was teetering on the edge.

In the solitude of his retreat,
on the days he was there, he
had good vibes within himself

and good vibes with the
headwaters of the wild river
and the springs that gushed
out from the mountainside.

He had done a noble thing,
having taken this risk, he had
experimented with truth itself,
like Gandhi, with Satyagraha.

XLVI

Solitary souls circle
Annapurna for love.

They sleuth on city streets,
and in cafes, churches.

Workmen with old clothes
and professionals with new
ask, Will there be love?
before they choose their partner.

Antonia's wide-eyed school-girl smile,
the flare of it,
the flash of it,
her slim body in a bloated world,
had erased the question primordially.

She was bipolar admittedly.
The conversation had bounced
like a red rubber ball nonstop,
right there on the dance floor,

from roommate rage and boyfriend fury
to doctors, medicines, anxiety at night.

Are you in college? asked Blaze.
I'm in and out, she said with a giggle.
If only I didn't need to work to keep
up my rent and help my mother too.

Then she told Blaze her private story
about her boyfriend and her roommate.

She sounded like a life boat
hovering on a tempetuous sea.

Or did she just say that
to ward off the subject?

Blaze looked on her like a father
and was drawn to her like a lover.

But he was no match for the younger men.

Was the athletic, handsome, preppy Korean
a lawyer, an engineer, a graduate student?

Blaze knew nothing about him except that
he, Blaze, was no competition for him.
Nor did the man seem to notice him at all.

Waiting this night, invisible in the crowd,
wearing dressy pants and blazer with an

open collar, he knifed into Blaze's nervous
approach diagonally at the cashier's desk,

taking Antonia by the hand to
dance in the zone behind the veil.

Old man Blaze slumped
humiliated behind the
ping-pong and pool
far back in the corner,

and Don't Know Much about History
and Bob Dylan's song If Not for You

played on for his listening pleasure.

He hoped that Mandy the waitress
hadn't seen him put down like that,
dwarfed, diminished, and bypassed,
as if he didn't count in that place.

Mandy, who always seemed to know
where he was and who he was with.

O, he counted alright.
Of this he had no doubt.

Lots of men looked at him, and
the starlets coveted his attention.

Be brave my heart, he said,
in the vehemence of the night.

Learn from the best of men, Murad Begh,
the bright, handsome, eloquent Mogul,
who you secretly watched and admired,

and his forced separation from Suniti Pal.
Her Brahmin family said No, it cannot be.

He was humiliated, but still passed
at the top of his class and began
his career with the United Nations.

Learn from the treasure at your feet,
the sagacious lesson of pure light, the

noble truth of the cause of suffering,
the noble truth of the soul's dark night,
the noble truth of the cloud of unknowing,

truths known of old
by mystics spurned
and magi scorned.

Then he fled outside to the canticle,
Brother can you spare some change.

XLVII

Who are you, hurting soul,
walking in the misty night
on the street in the lamplight,

through the laser beams
of parking lot attendants,

and under the flashing bulbs
of restored theaters, new classy
restaurants for emerging generations,
taco stalls and Mediterranean cafes,

the bright ribbons of neon streaming
down from the Stardust fortieth floor
and from the Galaxy across the street,

past the new construction of
upscale highrise apartments

with shiny new dark pavements
unlike the spotted and cracked
dusty white of the old sidewalk,

past the long lines of youth,
some having sat for hours, to
hear the current god of funk,

in a theater that had once shown
Gaslight and Sunset Boulevard
and The Old Man and the Sea,

you who give your heart and soul
to surpass your own worldedness
and exceed your own ordinariness?

Rivals be warned, though
he is no caped superhero,

and though the thin man
you see in common clothes
coming down the street
is not famous or rich,

he inhabits this and a higher world.

Though he carries no knife or gun, he
is armed with scratch paper and pen,

and atomic ideas that animate him
and move him forward into the day.

He comes with forgiveness,
with a mystical ontology,
with a Platonic metaphysics,

so that his pursuit is never-ending,
and guarded from idolatry and
mammon and the material mind.

Built by hubris, boasting ambition
of global empire and buried treasure
on island nations across the seas,

the towers vaunt their opposition
to the noble truth of renunciation.

They never give you their money,
they only give you their reputation.

Just this reveals their imperfection.

Local and contingent,
they cannot dwarf the one
who is poor in spirit,
hungry and thirsty for

righteousness, lonely for
perspective and new ideas,

the one who inherits the earth,
the one who breathes deeply
and seeks serenity under stress.

Fragmented and identified,
no match are they against
radical spiritual humility,

the oneness of humanity
above the things that divide us,

harmony with the wilderness,
compassion for suffering beings.

Behind the veil of
ignorance and desire,
they do not know what
awaits them, against

the one who can row from
Alcatraz across the currents
to the skyline of freedom.

XLVIII

Sometimes in his verses
Blaze Pascal spoke low.

Hang your head over,
hear the wind blow.

Be still and know,
like the grouse of
the desert grasslands
and the juniper forests.

She covers her brood
from the eyes of the bobcat,
the coyote, and the falcon.

The east lands of desert and pine
are now safe for the migration of
the tortoise and the bighorn sheep.

But when the train
leaves the station,
hear the wind blow.

Look out of the window
and see for yourself
the human empire grow.

The tent community on the
bridges across One-O-One,

documented and undocumented
migrants from south of the border,

mass crossings of borders everywhere,
immigrants leaving their livelihoods,

all victims of violence
and tyrannical regimes,

of agitated fragments,
smoldering clusters,
wanting identity.

The slums, the illiteracy,
they stretch as far
as the eye can see.

Look out of the window
and hear the wind blow.

See for yourself the junkyards,
the landfills, the factory farms,
the warehouses, the trucks.
See the human empire grow.

There is talk now of building a
wall in the Sonora Desert to
keep the undocumented away.

It will seal the fragmentation,
and it will divide and identify.

Who cares about the pronghorn herd,
their survival, their migration patterns?

Watch the armed gangs from
the Congo and South Sudan,
paid by organized crime.

See the elephants and rhinos
poached for the ivory trade,

snow leopards and the big cats
poached for their claws, teeth,
and so-called medicinal value.

All wildlife now
hunted to be eaten.

Its habitat degrades
and millions of
species go extinct.

Look at the sea animals,
when the train passes,

the factory farm animals, and
domesticated animals abused.

Note the rhino calf,
now abandoned,

the gorilla infant
left hungry,

the elephant baby
left circling
round its mother
on the ground.

XLIX

Blaze lived at the edge,
not quite knowing his
place in the world, not

at the church where he
convened his
religious dialogues, not

even at the Ground of Being,
where he was estranged from
the mainstream mind and
repelled by the hyperactivity,

though he had himself organized
philosophical dialogues on death,
mind, God, Marx, and religion.

He took his scratch paper and his pen
everywhere he went to jot down ideas.

He had them at lunch at Ground,
he had them sitting in libraries
and beachfront cafes, he had

them in Hollywood restaurants
and sitting under the Gary Cooper

portrait in Club Zero,
Do Not Forsake Me,
O My Darling
streaming in his soul.

He loved sitting there.
It was as if he was himself
was in that frontier town

with a desert stretching off
on all sides and expecting
the arrival of a train at noon

bringing the man who
had vowed to kill him.

He loved that song,
he loved that image

of the straight-ahead,
no-nonsense look of
Gary Cooper. He

loved the story of
courage and love

his and Grace Kelly's characters
portrayed in that classic western.

It was early at Club Zero, and
the main shift had not arrived.

Only Mandy the waitress walked over and
brought him the coffee he had asked for.

He gave her a tip and she blew him a kiss.
She had begun to like him for his big tips.
And he always asked her about her kids.

Then he jotted down the thoughts
that would later became his poetry.

In June the scorched earth
turned again to the north.

Then came the acorns
all polished, which once
I gathered and returned.

The evenings were cool.

Now the earth reverses its tilt
and the sun its waning warmth.

It is no mystery where the time goes.

It goes to adorn
the Brahmin princess
for her wedding.

Listen to the river flow that
comes from the eternal snow.

It comes to heal us of
our cancer and agitation.

Here we lay our burdens down.
This shall be our resting place.

When we assembled with Occupy
our chests swelled with hope.

The truth was so big, so old,
the message so plain, so bold.

When justice cries out in the streets,
surely the city will listen, we said.

When reason is heard in Contemplation,
surely the Council will answer Yes!

The Chambers were full.
The five men listened
because I used no notes, and
they had not seen me before.

We have waited for forty years, I said.
The mentally ill were left without care.

They withdrew the money. It
was the quality of their education.

The wind was not high,
the ocean was not deep,
the earth was not wide.

The horizons were fixed,
the stars a finite number.

Now are voices lifted in unison
for the homeless, the mentally ill.
How their numbers have grown!

The night is cold, we said.

L

Pray for us now and
in the hour of our death.

A man at the service,
Sugar Ray Lightfoot,
Black, bright, articulate,

homeless and brought
down by addiction,

in the Congregational Church courtyard, shaded
in the summer under its vines of bougainvillaea.

A homeless man had died
at Church and University
on the steps of City Hall.

Some said he had pneumonia, and
some he neglected his medicines.

One said he gave me a cigarette,
one praised him for his kindness.

We had marched through the streets
and stood here with our candles.

Bohemian and hippie in equal parts,
Sage Davies wore beads and bandanas
and had long light brown hair
that went well with her hazel eyes.

Her flamboyant dresses of unfathomable blue
with whorls and winds and moon at midnight
added to the mystique behind her madness.

Flashing in and out of our lives, she
was yet constant energy of Occupy
and brought students who joined us.

Quietly available, yet strange, unpredictable,
and when all was said and done, she
seemed isolated and discontent at the core.

She came to my back door
uninvited once, it was late.

We went for a Platonic walk
through the old cemetery and
the Garden of Ancient Trees,

where pines brushed the moon and
a coyote the chaparral, and oaks
cast shadows deeper than midnight.

We walked around the tall bare
chapel with sky blue chairs,

handsome wooden table in the
slightly raised front, and
narrow slits for the sun's rays.

It was bigger than my former cabin.
In the daytime when it was open
I went in for jotting down ideas.

We could hear the waters
from Mount Contemplation.

Her father had been a veteran.
She told me of her life shifting
between Japan and Hawaii and
across the San Francisco Bay.

Out of reach that night
was Signal Hill, where
Frank C. Laubach,
the Protestant mystic,

had heard the word on
humility and the oneness
of humanity beyond
the things that divide us.

I've heard of him, she said,
of his Each One Teach One.

I've seen his image on US
stamps. But no not this.
I had no knowledge of this.

I neither kissed her nor held her hand.
She had seen me as someone who
might companion her into the night
and perhaps beyond onto yonder shore.

Now she knew I was not the one.

Occupy endured the coldest months.
April came and scattered us, our

hearts a wild garden of spring desires
and ceaselessly expanding horizons,
portending new and ecological days.

LI

And the verses continued with this:

Backing up almost four months, I was
walking on cobblestone pathways
through redwoods and rhododendrons
and students lying reading on the grass,

when there came a sound of chanting
and commotion on University Street.

Everywhere we go....
people want to know....
What do we want?
JUS-TICE!....

It was the laid-off undocumented workers
whose soul voices had not gone unheard.

Concerned clergy and laypersons made
their presence known at the Posada later,

led by Father Sandoval Garcia
of the local Catholic church,

a thin long-nosed man with
rimless glasses, white robe, and
a stole from Central America.

It helped that he quoted Francis of Assisi
and a line from Pope Francis' Laudato Si.

Protestants were prominent too.
John Wieman, big muscular man
with a volcanic temperament,

respected for his long career of
advocacy for Hispanic workers.

He had a booming sonorous voice and
sang in the prestigious University Choir.

Milling around was an attractive clergywoman
with paper and pen asking for contact points.

We stood that day with the undocumented,
saying from campus station to campus station,

Is there sanctuary here?
The night is cold, we have
nowhere to lay our heads.

A young worker spoke to us
of her family in Angel City,
brothers, sisters, father, children.

She had stayed south to care
for their aging invalid mother.

Her stay here in this country was threatened
by the changing talk on immigration reform.

Her name was courage incarnate,
facing a system which had no face,

which had no heart,
which had no soul.

Who will come to San Ysidro with us?
Armed guards on the ground, in the air,
we will serve communion at the wire.

The call came from
church judicatories
in the City of Angels.

LII

To their food the bacteria swim.
At its nest the mockingbird sings.

In Tahrir Square the chant rings,
led once by a child of twelve,
which had glued me to the radio.

Life is the fair daughter
of goodness and word,
said of old to be lovers
from the beginning.

In the word is life,
and the life is the light.

Between the now and the not-yet
the redemptive idea is born.

This I learned at the seminary
north of the Golden Gate Bridge,

where I also read existentialism
and saw Sartre's play No Exit
in the round glassy Scott Hall,

led by Taylor Christian,
a slim, shy student with

a soft voice, brown eyes,
flashing red lipstick, and
an acute artistic drive.

Not a belief system, but art.
Art, the creation of beauty,

supplanted belief
as her religion,

just as philosophy,
the love of truth,
and mysticism,

can supplant belief
as one's religion.

Between hither and yonder
the star appears.
The way home is given in
a dream or in the first light.

Not in shallow meanings
growing in standing waters
is the way home given.

Religion is as unnecessary as tea,
said the gardener from her garden,

but ethics necessary like water, a
line, she said, from the Dalai Lama.

LIII

The prophet in the wilderness
proclaims the baptism of the river.

From the bog and the fog,
the gloom and the graveyard,
come to the river for the
amendment of your ways.

Be on the wavelength of the sea.

You can hear him coming,
the homeless man Rupert,

his hair undone,
reaching to the sky,
his eyes and his beard
as dark as his hair.

Sometimes he is high,
sometimes he is low.

His rasping dribble carries
through the Farmers Market,
the cafes and the restaurants,
indoor as well as outdoor.

He cannot listen,
he can only talk.

If you talk
he says listen.

Listen, he says,
do not interrupt.

Topanga Canyon,
Velveteen Rabbit,
the pub next to the station,
post-traumatic stress,

don't talk over me,
don't talk over me,
the Rolling Stones,

all I need is a dollar,
all I need is a dollar.

The sound rumbles through
the sidewalk like a train.
It smashes against the organ
before the service begins.

They offered him shelter.
He tried and could not.
They said hospitalization,
but he would not.

They tried to change the man,
but they did not understand.

They who understood
came down to the river,
to the cliffs and the caves,
for the amendment of their ways.

They came down to the
same wavelength as he,
the wavelength of the sea.

LIV

The coyote prowls at midnight.
We see nothing, we hear nothing.

It comes to take the cat, the rabbit, the
small dog, the fallen chicks of owls.
In the day it blends with all there is.

Agile and elegant,
patching and peeling,
it glides on city streets.

It knows the oleander,
the garden foliage,

the back spaces,
the restaurant alleys,
the garbage bins.

Today I walk like the coyote
along the dry creek and the
willows in the white rock ravine
of blue blade and purple sage.

The old fir higher up
protested the wind
swishingly in December.

Now it calls in whispers.

From the pavement
come to the path
that leads to the pond.

From contortion
come to clarity.

From compulsion
come to calm.

No langurs leaping in deodars
against the eternal snows,

no Gurkhas traveling to the mountain city
through Sisters Bazaar to release their loads,

no missionaries gathering to sing
in Kellogg Church on Landour Ridge.

Yet these mountains rising
and these landslides sliding,
this fir dust, cone, and deadwood,

bid the same leaping freedom,
the same release of burdens,
and the same hymns that soar

above the absurdity of
feasting in a violent world,

above the age of
cancer and compulsion,

above the dread
of having nothing to do
and nowhere to go,

of being duped
by mad leaders
into war,

by solipsistic guides
down the wrong road.

LV

I climb higher and
the ravine darkens,
the chaparral thickens,
the music deepens.

Water drips percussively
upon ancient rocks.

Among these mountains
I am afraid,
alone and away
from the blue highway.

Here there is life,
here there is death.

Invisible eyes watch me
through the thickets
of oak, pine, and sycamore.

Something has slept here
under the manzanita, mahogany,
and fifty other nameless shrubs,

the wet leaves pressed
down and glowing red.

Was it a moose?
A mountain lion?
What did I disturb?

Questions so intimate,
so private as this,
are surely forbidden.
Surely I trespass.

Among the cactus
I reach my limit.

Fallen trees lying
across mammoth boulders,

their trunks jagged
with savage points,
the broken bones below,

they belong to
the bear and the bobcat,
the sheep and the snake,
the cougar and the coyote.

I did return what
I took in September,

acorns, stones, twigs,
a fallen fragment
of a cedar limb,

like the pebbles that lay
on my table for thirty years,
which I returned to the sea.

LVI

La Cienega the name is a little song, as
are Grauman's Chinese and San Bernardino.

Hear me say Santa Monica Boulevard and
you will hear the undercurrents of the sea.

At Club Zero I paid the
cashier the entrance fee.

I had known Maria from
Roseland, long closed.
She joked about old men, and
no love was lost between us.

Peaceful Easy Feeling was playing.
I stood still for the best of the Eagles.
I loved that song, more than Lying Eyes.

It had made a resurgence during the Iraq War,
which went with ...*against your skin so brown.*
I want to sleep with you in the desert tonight.

George W was a good man,
though immature, I felt, and
this was reflected in his choice
of colleagues, one of whom

would breathe vengeance,
another braggadocio, and
another a warped ideology
into his Oval Office.

I sat down by the old Japanese man who
had been introduced to me as Peter.

He knew little English
and wore hearing aids.

He was about my age. We nodded.
He complained again about the prices.

Do you feel the same way? he asked.
No, I said, I find them quite reasonable.

He could not hear, but he
understood my gestures.

I offered to buy him coffee
when the waitress appeared.
No, I do not drink coffee.

I had known Mandy before too,
back from when she was a dancer.
Now we flirted only at the counter.

Again Peter started dozing and was
tapped on the shoulder by a guard.

We were sitting at a table with
white-and-red-striped tablecloths
under the old chandeliers.

Some Enchanted Evening sent
me into a World War 2 movie,
From Russia with Love
into a Cold War spy movie.

I watched for Antonia to
emerge from the plastics
of the pastels of autumn,

yellow against green and rust
and the black of tree limbs.

She was not only attractive but
seemingly happy with everyone,

the handsome Korean professional,
the Chinese doctor, who now stood
at the desk waiting for her appearance,
who was also a presence at the Abyss,

young men, old men, disabled men,
some who knew each other well,
men with sneakers and Lakers sweats,
men with suits and polished shoes.

Three handsome pleasant Hispanic
males looked like gang members.

Not to worry about my medicines,
only about my anxiety at night.

It was late when we danced.
Up close I could feel her disease,

the upside breathing in my face,
the conversation a thrown stone
bouncing over the water.

I never saw the downside,
reserved for the shadows,
when the city was asleep.

Do you plan on finishing college?
Again I asked the epic question,
and again Antonia equivocated.

Was it I alone who knew?
Was it I alone who cared?

I told no one of my visits
to the city of private
detectives and dancing girls.

No one would understand.

LVII

A misty drizzle had filled the air, and
construction lights slowed the traffic.

The world was in flux and reflux,
like the moon, like the sea, and

Club Zero was the paradigm of impermanence.

Many came,
many left.

I had seen time itself withdraw,
wallow, waver, and withdraw.

The club was a tidal wave,
having gone through changes
for over forty years from

throngs of jostling men and women
to a much leaner and meaner style.

To surf the wave,
surpass the wave,
before the sea subsides,

this became my mantra.

Antonia had equivocated,
turning away from me,

her disorder pulling at
her native intelligence,

her disease tearing
her sanity apart.

Can turning away ever fetch love?
The question reechoed within me.

LVIII

Blaze Pascal continued
writing into his old age.

It had been nine years
since he came to
the Ground of Being
and started his verses.

The extended drought had worried us.
It had been the topic of talk at the table.

Then the rain brought snow to the mountains,
and the water gushed white in the drains.

Not for a paper ship, that water.
Not for a contemplative old soul
who had to jump across the streams

on his way to the university library
and then back to his home at Ground.

The juniper was blowing in the window.
I knew most of the activists in the room,

retired professors,
specialists some on water,
some in ecology,
some in organic agriculture,

and church workers from around the globe,

fifteen to twenty persons
crowded in a small space,

meeting to organize a conference
on climate change and
the deteriorating environment.

New was Singing Moon and her friend,
who said she also croons Billie Holiday.

Love for the earth is the
religion of my people.

She said this quietly
when a space occurred,
but it wasn't heard.

The talking was avid, and
her words were whelmed
by egos ineluctable,
anxious themselves to be heard,

and quite unaware that
the winter of wolves
had entered the room.

It had bothered me from the start.
People talking over each other,
the shallow level of the conversation,
final decisions being made only by

my friend Plump Graybeard,
whose real name was Bill Oliver,
retired from Yale Divinity School.

I had come to know Bill well and
teased him about his waistline and
dusky Mediterranean complexion.

He had taken over leadership from our ailing
chair, whose vision yet drove the planning.

Bill's systematic theology, loaded
with a high Christology and a
belabored theology of God, was

still a mid-twentieth century expression,
a point of endless debate between us,

though it was received uncritically as
cutting edge by so many in the church.

His decisions on worship were
hurried and insipid, and on music
joyless, mediocre, unoriginal.

Stay, Singing Moon, sing
I Cover the Waterfront.

Tell us the I-Thou religion
of the path in the woods

that leads to the waterfall and
to the headwaters of the river,

of the nurse logs that decay
and give birth to all there is.

Speak of the fire
that burns your soul

when you hear the search
of the angry breeze.

The shifting fire and
the stolen fallen trees.

LIX

This was written in
the Mean Streets Cafe.

The main floor of the
Wilshire One Tower.

Fateful crossing of
esteemed worlds.

Careers at stake,
no time to think.

Friday afternoon.
Almost alone, I
was sitting and pacing
in the Mean Streets Cafe,

scouring the intersection
for a classy young starlet

with deep brown smiling eyes
and soft round features,

who could be elusive,
who could be giving.

A Hispanic man was also there
with his little daughter
scampering among the tables.

He too seemed to be waiting.

Sahara had suggested this cafe.
She had reappeared at the Abyss

and was preoccupied with
entrepreneurs, business men,
professionals in law and medicine.

I saw a therapist giving her a shoulder
massage in the television sitting area.

She was in no mood to dance
with a philosophical old man,

and gave me the cold shoulder
as she walked by to dance
with another man waiting,

though later she let me hold her
on the dance floor glowing red.
I told her how pretty she was and

snuggled with her, caressed her,
behind the Chinese artsy screens,
draped lattices, tropical plants.

Yet a coldness attended our dance
on both of our parts, even as she
told me of the Mean Streets Cafe.

And the DJ played Sinatra,
From Here to Eternity, from

the film of the same name,
starring Burt Lancaster,
Deborah Kerr, Montgomery
Cliff, and Sinatra himself.

Sahara had been believable,
I thought, like water, and
had been right, like rain.

Now even as we danced
that ambiguous angry night,
the question What shall I do?
clawed at me like a feral cat.

Do I burn the bridge between us? No,
I would not give her that much power.

I would wait for the tide.
I needed air to breathe.

And I was in no position to burn the bridge.

I would choose the middle path,
the zone between belief and unbelief,
the street between freedom and love.

LX

Two hours had passed.
No sign of Sahara.

I was still alone, except
for the Hispanic man and
his lovely little daughter.

Insurance and real estate agents,
advertisers and graphic artists,
dentists and dental assistants,

secretaries and receptionists,
lawyers, judges, and legal staff,
government and corporate officials,

all trafficked through security,
and used the elevators nonstop.

Some actually rushed into the cafe for
an energy, nutrition, or gluten-free bar.

I watched the sweet child,
lost in her own world, the
universe of chairs and tables.

She knew her father's fortifications,
the meaning of his motionlessness.

Foreboding was in his posture,
and fear in his vacant eyes.

Would they take the child away?
Where was the child's mother?
Did she work upstairs in the tower?

I pondered these things in
Mean Streets that afternoon,
watching the world go by.

Soon it would be five, and the
persons in the tower would be
free to join the Friday rush
hour and drive to their release.

It was irony, it was paradox,
the divinity of the rush hour,
its germ being this knowledge,

knowledge that it was Friday, and
the end of strife was in clear view.

The end of stress,
the end of strain,
the end of grind,

the end of putting up,
the end of pent-up,
the end of obedience.

Bumper to bumper the
persons of the tower
know what they will do.

Their hearts will race even
if they themselves cannot.

The day will glow even
if the sky itself is gray.

The multiplex and the popcorn,
the television shows and the chips,

will deal a blow to the loneliness.

The shopping malls and restaurants,
the clubs and concerts and alcohol,
will hold boredom at arm's length.

The child I watched dulled
her own unconscious pain
playing among the tables.

The father was blanked out
and staring at nothing at all.

LXI

Blaze Pascal jumps no more
from boulder to boulder
in Contemplation Creek.

He finds a softer place.
He keeps a slower pace.

He does not walk alone in
labyrinths of tumbled rock.

He avoids the extremes.
He finds a middle path,

which is the journey itself
between hither and yon,

the sacred space itself,
between ground and abyss.

His church, he says, is an
orbiting, turning, tilting thing,

tilting between idea and time,
between word and world,
between essence and existence.

We are an amorphous community,
open, porous, inclusive, uncertain.

Open independent dialogue,
the in-between-ness of truth,
the dialogue itself as wisdom,
this is our conviction.

We break the bread and say,
We are one with suffering beings,
endangered animals everywhere,

kidnapped women and children,
migrants and immigrants,
documented and undocumented,

persecuted minorities,

the LGBTQ community,
Muslims threatened
with hate letters

from an address in
the City of Angels.

Ahimsa, nonviolence,
the creation and preservation
of beautiful things,
this is our worship.

We have no ritual of membership.

All who support the church,
all who seek to free the soul
from ignorance and violence,
are members of the church.

LXII

Wading in the sea Blaze watched a
little girl of seven with big brown
eyes play with her small flat board,

laying it down at the edge,
standing on it, and waiting
to see what would happen
when the sea came in.

She did this again and again.
She was consumed by it.
She looked only for the sea.

He sat down in the sand and
wrote down the thoughts
that he would expand later.

At Point Conception
I am in my church.

I am at the edge,
the edge of a rock
overlooking the sea.

On a clear day,
I can see forever.

We are a common humanity,
standing on common ground,

avowing a common faith,
beyond the things that divide us.

I hear wind chimes playing
2-note and 3-note and
abstract multi-note songs.

I see Paul Tillich swimming
far out in the ocean of being.

I see him looking up
and waving at me
standing on the rock.

Won't you come and join
me, he calls, in the
breaking of the waves and
the dialectic of the sea?

Yes, I reply gladly, I will join you
in the breaking of the theological
waves, the dialectic of the sea,
and the controversy of life.

He disappears and reappears as I watch.

The existentialism of
alienation and angst,
ground and abyss, and

the inexhaustible
depth of being,

and of the courage to be
in the face of nonbeing,

were his contribution
to the theological and
cultural hermeneutic,

and for this he drew crowds
for his public lectures and
for his university seminars.

I heard cosmic fluctuations,
atomic explosions, deep
underneath the ground, and
reverberations all around,

a shaking of the foundations theologically.
Nothing would be the same ontologically.

I have been grateful for the
example of his own courage
when it was not popular
in the theological academy.

Familiar figures strolling
on the beach and along the
Loop Trail, crunchy soft with
mesquite berries and pinefall,

they appeared and disappeared.

Gandhi and C.F. Andrews,
and Mother Teresa in white.

There was truth in her doubts.
It was good she told of them.

Rosa Parks said No in Alabama,
evincing the courage of being.

Thomas Merton, the Trappist monk.
He used the Sinai myth to render the
mysticism of the soul's dark night
and the cloud of unknowing:

Clarity at the foot of the mountain,
in the white desert sand, and
thunder, lightning, monsoon mist,
as we climb higher and higher.

Will you walk with us? they ask.
Yes of course, I say, I have
learned much from your example.

I will follow behind you,
always watching the sea,
listening to the waves and
the wind in the trees.

Boethius the philosopher,
who wrote The Consolation
of Philosophy, awaiting his

execution while imprisoned
by the Ostrogoth Theodoric,

he too passed by and asked,
Will you join me on
the road to Consolation,

though many dangers lie
ahead for us on that road?

Yes, I said, I have read your
book in the seminary library,
and will certainly join you
on the road to Consolation,

though I am not brave like you,
and I too may be imprisoned to

await my execution by
fragmented, finite minds,
idolotrous, worlded minds.

I will be watching the sea
and listening to the waves
and the wind in the trees.

Alonzo Church and Gottlob Frege,
two philosopher logicians,
were walking on the beach
and swimming in the sea of light.

E. J. Lemmon was just behind them
and joined them from time to time.

They looked up and waved.

Many, many others came by,
so many I lost count of them,
who had been an example of
goodness in a degraded world,

whose beams had shone out
to a turbulent sea and had guided
many a ship safely to shore,

some who died ingloriously,
some who languished in prisons dark,
some who suffered abuse excessively,
and no one knew or came to help.

Let it not be said,
as cynics say in the city
to dismiss religion,

There lie the dead bones
of the human soul.

No, no, no, no!
To nurture and not to cling,

to teach the courage to be
in the face of nonbeing,
and then let be and let go,

this is life, not death.

To exist in the passion
between the now and the not-yet,
in this is mystic wisdom,

denied by our cultured despisers.

LXIII

Do not look for closure
or a fixed conclusion.

Inherit the earth
turning, turning, and
tilting north and south.

Consider the sea
tossed by waves
rising and falling,

and the sky
so big, so blue,
penetrated by the
blackness beyond.

A village flute
would come to me
after lights-out,

high but not shrill,
subservient to
the dark unknown,

after Miss Lawie's
piano had galloped
upon the mountains,

signifying victory
over the unknown,
as I lay sleeping.

The flute sounded far, far away, though
it really came from the servants' quarters.

Once I saw a blue heron
circling for its mate,
hoping against hope,
and fearing the worst.

Be with me for
the coral reefs,
the rain forests,

the gray wolf,
and the red fox.

Bring many names of
wild lands and waters,

and animals endangered,
extinct, abandoned,
poached, and farmed.

The Sufis have ninety-nine names.

Overhung by palms,
oaks, and sycamores,
the pond has no words,

yet the algae and fungi,
the bees and the dragonflies,

the tadpole things in the water,
known by their perfect circles,
which shatter against other worlds,

offer their consolation. They
know the shooting momentum
of our flight upon the waves,

and the dazzle of our wings,
only an ephemeral point in
the fabric of space and time.

The circles, fervent in the summer,
in a pond of shaded broccoli green,

are now serene
in the pale blue
of the winter sky.

LXIV

And the poetic verses of
Blaze Pascal continued
with this episode in the
Creative City of Angels.

The Brahmaputra was crowded
and noisy this evening, with

Bollywood songs filling the air
and children pulling on saris.

The man behind the counter served me
dal and rice, charging me little, after

I began leaving him bigger tips, saying,
after I saw him smoke outside,
This is not for cigarettes: It is
for your wife, children, and yourself.

I spoke mostly Urdu at the restaurant.

After the dal and rice,
after the chai and sweets,

I worked my way down
Santa Monica, then
Normandy to Wilshire,
and then to Club Zero,

and stood with the lonely men watching
the gossiping and giggling dancing girls
in short skirts and current fashions.

I stood contemplative
among the likes of

Paquiao and Salvador Sanchez,
Carlos Monzon and Marquez.

When contemplative
we search the faces
for the depth of being,

for love and the forms
of being in the world.
We listen for the tone.

When contemplative
we breathe deeply and
gather our strength to be
in the face of nonbeing.

We are restrained
and fear no evil

in the dining hall,
on the mean street,
in the busy junction.

The clock that hung
once upon a time
above the mantlepiece

seventy years ago in a city
across the river from Lahore

now hangs behind my eyes and
oscillates between power and control.

My Bultmann existentialism
demythologizes my dancing,

and marks in bold
strokes the groundlessness
of the place itself.

Under the portrait of Gary Cooper
I withdraw into the
mysticism of the soul's dark night.

LXV

Let Antonia learn her own lessons!
Come to your senses, Blaze Pascal!

You are not her lover!
You are not her father!

You are not the one,
the one they call
the Seventh Son.

She is manic and metropolitan,
her room is multitudinous,
and she is bright and witty,
and bouncy like a rubber ball.

She has her father,
she has her mother.
She is close to them,
she speaks of them.

She will lean on them, and will
draw from her own experience,
and she will find her own way.

Let Sahara sit with other men!
She knows best what is good!

Inhabit your age, old man!
Your love is not requited!

Sahara is shrewd and self-assured,
her room is fastidious,
and she is patient and perceptive.

The Chinese doctor,
with whom she sits,
is calm and cool
and contemporary.

He takes emergency calls on the dance floor,
walking away from his partner to answer them,
sometimes taking the elevator up at the Abyss.

He drives a spaceship
tentacled for the moon,
and for the moons
beyond the moon.

Walk away, Blaze Pascal.
Listen to the word within.

Even the music, a melange
of raucous Tijuana colors,
hastens your flight from
the soldiers of Herod.

Thus it was that I went home
and told no one of my nights

in the megalopolis of music,
mean streets, and movie stars.

LXVI

Sitting among the stacks
in the seminary library
Blaze Pascal did not tire

of telling his story, driven
ultimately by his own ideas,

and which would not be read,
he knew, for a long, long time.

The next evening I was invited to a meeting in
which Dr. Morton Donaldson would present.
I had read and even met the man decades ago.

No one had posed the question of emptiness
like he did in the Hartshorne living room
before fifteen of us gathered that evening.

It would scandalize moral feeling.

No one had asserted the banality of boredom quite
as explosively as the man did, toting the triumph
of Babylon, mother of all harlots and abominations.

Boredom is despised above all things.

Idiocy, he scoffed, is taken for comedy,
garish gloss for graphic art, and metal
monsters for suspense in the cinema.

The surreal visitor
from Armageddon,
his hair undone
and fire in his eyes,

expounded his new book on
the apocalypse of God, and

the death of meaning,
the contemporary
spiritual nightmare.

God is dead!
The soul is expired!
The spirit has
breathed its last!

This is the end.

Has it come this? he said:
Terror in the name of religion,

the mass flight across borders
of men, women, and children,

the earth itself at risk
by human overpopulation?

I noticed his young secretary's classy
college face and her modest gray suit.

Four of the theologians rightly recoiled,
hearing this onslaught against theology,
and made sincere efforts at rejoinder.

Lanky, handsome man
was Matthew, with
dark, flashing eyes and
hard, pointed features,

and learned in many religions,
a married man with children.

Kenneth D. Stephens

He was the first theologian
to respond, and he argued
that the world's soul cries
out against its own decline.

I myself, he said, have called
the faithful here to prayer
with an Eastern chant based

on the Maha Mritrityunjaya,
using the flute and the sitar.

These sublime calls to prayer
and the earnestness of the chants,
calling the heavens, the skies,
the earth, the waters, the herbs,

and humans to peace and love,
belie the apocalypse of
which you speak so awesomely.

Mark, the second theologian, a
heavy man with a heavy voice
and rimless glasses, well-dressed,

visiting professor from Heidelberg,
spoke with a pronounced accent.

He reminded the circle of
his own reintertpretations

of existential meaning
beneath the madness
and behind the absurd.

Death of meaning? No!
Even the mad hermit
of Red River, who

sleeps under a bridge,
uses drugs, eats garbage,

collects cans and bottles
and empty cigarette packs,

explains he can live no
longer in a judgmental
and behavioristic world.

Yes, what is madness but a lunge
from the Bridge of No-Understanding
into the River of Deeper Meaning,

a sad, short, ragged life, chosen freely
against ignorance and violence?

I speak, he said, of the same lunge that
plummeted Kierkegaard into his faith.

We heard echoes too of Jean Paul Sartre,
Martin Heidegger, and Simone de Beauvoir.

Luke was the third, a thin, bald,
energetic man with a strong voice
for his years, an actual nerd, a
brilliant retired theologian, who

I saw walking his dogs daily,
both procured from the pound.

He adored his dogs, and
no one one was prettier
than Sapphire and Sage!

He admitted the failure of theology
to speak to its cultured despisers
on their own philosophical terms.

But we are far from finished.
This lack of contemporaneity,

he said, was just what my own
later work and even my current
efforts have essayed to address.

But Luke, my friend, said John,
the fourth theologian, interrupting,
while I respect your basic concern,
you collude with modernity, you

sacrifice religion's claims on the
human heart and mind on the altar
of applause by the modern assembly.

I myself seek no such affirmation,
but stand by my Anselmic proof in
the logic of possibility and necessity.

By my proof, already in print,
the voice of Babylon is silenced.

John looked pale from his recent surgery.
He had also just lost his wife to cancer.

He had visited her daily right up to the end,
and was there when she breathed her last.

A neo-classicist, well-known academically,
his ontological proof used Anselm's axiom,
If God exists, then God exists necessarily.

LXVII

After the exchange with Donaldson, the
theologians' talk drifted and degenerated
into sloven and solipsistic chatter about
publishing their own correspondence.

I did not know Matthew well, but had
heard of his recent academic conflicts.

I did not know Mark at all, but grew
quite interested in his existentialism.

I knew and liked Luke and John,
fellow residents with me at Ground.

But confronted with an impasse
of such weight and magnitude,
the theologians sounded dull.

And I found no significance
in the present conversation.

I grew impatient,
excused myself, and
walked out into the dark.

The day was now far spent.
It had not yet begun to rain.

And as I walked I wondered
about Donaldson, what

tribulation he had endured,
this man of over ninety years.

Long ago we had disagreed, he
with his postmodern relativism,

and I searching to be constructive
in my philosophical activity.

It was not good for my career,
not in an analytic environment,
to experiment that way, but I

followed the tug of my thoughts.
And thoughts led on to thoughts
like ways lead on to ways.

Now as I heard him I still had no
sympathy with his worldedness,

which was leading only to nihilism
and indeed to his apocalypticism.

The world did not need a prophet
who had nothing positive to say,
who saw nothing good in the world,

no hope,
no truth,
no love,
no beauty,

nothing sacred or transcendent
to replace his Babylonianisms.
He had not changed over time.

So easy it is to channel one's life
into a purpose less than worthy!

Where was the voice of reason,
which embodies itself in us and

shows the way of kindness
toward all suffering beings,

the way of freedom
from all things and
for all things, the

way of wisdom, which
is the love of beauty,
the soul of the world?

If only he would suddenly have
had a change of heart and mind!
Had become a different prophet!

And called the city to the river
for the amendment of its ways,

to the knowledge that transcends the
flattened, fragmented, finite mind and
the way one pronounces shibboleth!

Even his young secretary had spoken up
of the folk songs of the youth in Denver.

They sing, she said, of hope overcoming
despair, of perfect love casting out fear.

I paused under a gigantic deodar,
breathing deeply the fragrant air,

and looking back watched the mist
drift among the trees under the lamp.

LXVIII

Snow had been falling on my head from
the aspen and big-leaf mountain maples.

Now I was out in the open. The
expanding whiteness was all in all.

Radiant crown on the
precipitous height
beaming a holy light,

beauty the color of wind and fire
sweeping across the slopes,

peace, like the dust, rubble,
and stone beneath the snow,
the ground on which I walked.

To breathe the air of
the purple sage, the
pine, the manzanita,
is to breathe life itself.

The pleasures of the earth
and the passions of the soul,
let us affirm them both as one.

Do I elevate matter
and denigrate spirit?

No no no no, I do neither!

Though distinct in idea,
in the world all passion,
even of the soul, seeks
actualization in pleasure.

The ideal seeks its occurrence
or reoccurrence in the world.

Beauty seeks creativity,
love desire,
freedom responsibility,
truth its telling in the world.

Names conjoined on sprawling oaks
and raptures told on ancient boulders prove
the inseparability of love and pleasure.

But come with me under the
bridge over Contemplation Creek,
and read with me the poetry.

See pleasure and bliss
rise and fall united
on the scribbled wall.

Hear flesh and spirit crash and flow,
a single stream under the willows.

The stream takes us to the
sea lest we get stranded.

There we see them circle,
the fins of finite knowledge,
the jaws of jealous minds.

Bitten we hasten and
draw yet nearer to the
shore of unknowing
engulfed in the mist.

There we shall gather the
strength and courage to be.

LXIX

I stood today between
death and resurrection,

the one in last year's apologetic gray,
the other arrayed in bracing pink.

Old things are passing away:
All things are becoming new.

Today Sahara sits with the Chinese doctor.

They will surely exceed each
other in the fullness of time.

She is acquisitive, opaque, discreet,
he contemporary, precise, discriminating.

Will love prevail at high noon,
when the arrow flies by day?

And will love yet be faithful
when pestilence strikes in the dark?

LXX

Antonia, slender and transparent, tells of
her symptoms in her hands and sensations.

It always happens on
the dance floor that
I want to dance close,

and she wants to talk, and it's
usually about her family and
social life and her disabilities.

Are you taking your meds? I ask.
The doctors are changing my meds,
she says, and I've been tired helping
my mom pay rent and clean house.

Do you visit your father
at the Los Angeles Port?

Not at the Port, no, he's way too busy there, but
I'm close to him and worried about his love life.

I don't know if his new
girlfriend is working out.

A John Denver song
comes like a gust of
wind and carries me
to a night in a forest.

Antonia expresses no interest in music,
judging from the way she dances,
no hint of rhythm in her movements,
too young anyway to know John Denver.

Antonia is not a liar,
though I waited in vain
in the Pike Place Diner,
listening to the foghorns.

A prodding parent and prancing child
walked hand in hand down the street.

The place was grungy. I looked
out towards the ships and the sea,
which I had traveled so long ago.

A pretty American woman, among
hundreds of Asian students, had
been on the President Cleveland.

I noticed her right away
and saw her looking at me.

The dining hall, the corridors,
even the moonrise on the deck,
these grow dim now in memory,

but her face against the open sea
looms large within my mind.

I knew in my heart
she was drawn to me,
and that she knew
I was drawn to her.

Once she and her friend
were sitting on the steps.
I passed between them,
and again she stared at me.

I brought to these shores
nothing at all, but my

cantankerous philosophical
and theological quest
and these feelings for her.

And that I am shy on the deck,
shy coming down the steps, and
that I send the wrong vibrations.

LXXI

Blaze Pascal, divided in himself
about religion, and having
long obsessed about it, had come

to this, that it's better that
the poetry absorb the plot,
and the song the story.

Give us Barabbas!
Give us Barabbas!

It was the Chorale in
unison in Disney Hall.

In Lent a homilist at Ground
did not indulge the narrative,
but opted to sing A Lily Blooms
in the Cold Gloom of Spring,

conveying the message eloquently,
hope in these times of uncertainty,
light for the streets of darkness,
grace and love in the age of terror.

Kenneth D. Stephens

Yes, thought Blaze Pascal,
when he beheld the drama,

to be led this way into
paths of truth and light.

Belief yielding to feeling,
like music theory to sound,
the literal to the mystical,

like the teacher
to what is taught.

Our own bodies given for
the liberation of the world,

our own blood poured out for
the healing of hurting beings.

A hush fell on receptive hearts.
Those who walked in darkness
saw the aurora in the first beams.

Those who dwelt in the land of shadows
saw the great red sea of eastern clouds.

Old man Blaze told his conclusions
to only a few in table conversation.

Some changed the subject
when the idea soaked in.

Adelia M did not want to
deal with it, not at lunch.
Some said nothing at all.

He told his private life
to no one at Ground.

LXXII

Blaze Pascal knew himself to
be more post-religious than
religious or non-religious,

more post-theist than non-theist,
more post-secular than secular.

The winter solstice came and went.
Christmas came and went, with its
carols and pageants and services.

He kept his distance but
heard about them at table.

Have yourself a merry little Christmas,
he said to the social world around him.

It struck a chord within him,
that Martin and Blane song,
made famous by Judy Garland
in Meet Me in St. Louis.

He picked up a note of sadness
between its lines of cheer, recalling
the happy golden days of yore.

Some day soon our troubles will
be out of sight: Until then
we'll muddle through somehow.

So true, thought the old man, as he walked
alone in the streets under gray skies,
looking up at snow-capped Contemplation,

stopping at a tree that had showered
him with leaves last Christmas Day,
but this time had only a few left
among its clumps of small red berries.

The stillness and silence washed over him.
Walking alone was good for him for now,
and allowing himself the skyline of the city.

He was happy that having muddled
through, he had reached this point,
though he still had muddling to do.

Muddling is never-ending, he knew,
but he had made some good choices
together with the bad along the way.

Breathing in capitalism and
breathing out individualism,

we embraced the consolation of the song,
we who were muddling through now with

drugs, diseases, and divorces, with
family and financial problems, with

living with the consequences of
the dumb decisions we've made.

Peace and joy and sadness all
found their place in his heart.

That winter Blaze Pascal
was asked to offer grace,
and this is what he said.

I heard a voice saying,
Take off your thirsty boots
and stay for a while.

Come to the table, partake
of this bread of wisdom,
courage, and compassion.

Then the voice said, Cry!
And I said, What shall I cry?

Cry to the four winds for the
deported pregnant woman,
and for the land riven where
the jaguar prowls for food.

LXXIII

Fresh snow had appeared
on Mount Contemplation
and cold air had settled
in the Valley of Angels.

Robed students at the gates of the mammonic city
shook their heads at the dense streets before them.

What they saw was absurdity.

The best would seek sophia,
the word from the river,
the sea, and the wilderness,

and their goals be basic,
like running water,
their work instinctive,
like the will to live.

Some will advance their learning.
One will first go to teach in Nepal.

Some will be submerged in the monsoon
that creeps up the ravines from nonbeing.

At graduation Contemplation
is crowded with
families and noisy children,

young couples with roller boards,
and bicyclists from everywhere, waiting
in line in the cafes and restaurants.

Music unknown to this new generation played that
day unheard above the commotion in Platonic Coffee.

Nothing's gonna change my world.
Nothing's gonna change my world.

At the counter sat Blaze Pascal writing
another grace he would offer at noon.

Brando in The Godfather,
Bergman and Bogart
in Casablanca,

Redford and Streisand
in The Way We Were,

and John Lennon at the piano
looked down upon him.

Jai Guru Deva.

Past, present, and future, three
concentric circles in a pond.

And in the alley three crows
flew away at his approach.

LXXIV

I lift my eyes to the hills.
How sacred they are, and
holy the bridegroom sun
and the cycles of the moon.

The injured rocks murmur
of times long gone, and
they deserve our respect.

The lemur and the leopard,
the langur and the orangutan,

all living things take delight
in their existence,
and cry out for our concern.

Even the philosopher, in the John Dewey Lecture, affirmed
the imperative of preventing needless suffering as an absolute.
He said this to a hall-full of postmodern faculty and students.

Blaze Pascal had once been stopped, on a
winding highway from the snow and stars,

by a grouse and her chicks, who would
not move from the middle of the road.

He got out to shoo them away,
and he had wondered for long
if it was necessary to do so.

It was necessary to do so.

LXXV

The skyline was charcoal,
floating in fire and gold, as the
sun went down into the sea.

Faces against the panes,
Paquiao versus Marquez,
pigeons changing perches,

palms waving, Come to the sea
and walk among the stars.
Come to the Boulevard and walk
where the stars have walked.

But Blaze Pascal paid them no heed.
It was, ah, the girl who had said,
Good karma there is between us,
it was with her he had come to dance,

to dance with her in the corners,
to snuggle with her in the dark,
on the privileged side of the veil.

Shall he say,
Impermanence
rules the city?

Shall he say, Essence
is prior to existence?

Shall he say, The voice said Cry,
and I said What shall I cry?

No, but this, this is
what he shall say,

Whisper to me this night,
though the music is loud.

No one can hear, and
no one else is near.

Hold me close,
it will not be for long.

What will she say?
She will be thinking
about the money she
must make this night.

Anxiety, he knew,
stalks in the night
this blithe and manic
cosmopolitan maiden.

A room-mate, a boyfriend,
driven away,
money-changers chased
from the temple of her room,

Antonia thinks and texts
at the speed of light.

How long will she withstand
the scourge of her disease?

How long will her own
karma hold good in the city,
she who had said at first
sight, We have good karma?

How long will she refuse
the discipline of college?

The questions pressed upon him both in real
time and when the time had gone, when the
young man had taken his place behind the veil.

LXXVI

Hear the wind blow, love,
hear the wind blow.
Hang your head over,
hear the wind blow.

The ways of the world lead to dead ends.

Blaze Pascal fled to the desert.
The desert understood him and
his unfitness in the world, though
he wanted and needed the world.

There he reached high for the
courage of being in the world,

to face the contradiction of that,
the tension of being and world,
the polarity of ideal and actual.

Blaze Pascal fled to the mountains.
The mountains understood his need
to transcend the waters of nonbeing,

to look objectively upon the world
and his own need for the world.

To both I-and-It with the world
and I-and-Thou with the world.

Down in the valley
he heard the wind blow.
On the banks of the river
he laid his burdens low.

Old soul Blaze fled to the sea.
The sea understood him and
his need to shut out the world,
though he loved the world.

There he heard the word
from the bottom of the sea,
the consolation of philosophy.

There as the waters lapped against his knees,
he reached for the strength to be in the world,

to face the opposition of being and world,
to live into the polarity of ideal and actual.

Tomorrow perhaps we will play
with you in the moonlight.
We are fixed tonight on our slates
with arithmetic, and the school
master is strict and demanding.

Kenneth D. Stephens

Tomorrow we will pull turnips
together when the gardener is asleep.
The evening has stolen by like thief.

LXXVII

Blaze Pascal's secret nights
continued in the big city,
again at the Abyss, where

Sahara sat with the Chinese doctor
and with other professional men
with suits, ties, and shiny shoes, in

the building of the Kienholz tableau,
Back Seat Dodge 1938, from the
Whitney Museum of American Art,
high above the busy parking lot.

There he danced with a goddess,
come in the guise of a Tajik princess.

Innocence was in her bearing, and
she was eager to know this man.

Earnest was her question, What
philosophy book should I read?

The chords of Skyfall acquiesced,
and the silken dress shed
its perfume and silver sheen,

as he groped in vain to answer
the query of a pristine mind

in a place as inimical as this

to the nudge of exalted thought.

He was aware of no simple books,
and philosophy he knew must be
learned in a classroom setting.

Chastened by such purity of heart, and after
tipping and returning her to the cashier and
paying for the twenty minutes they had spent,

privately he asked himself,
What evil spirit drives me
to these libidinous nights?

Shush, he answered,
do not be harsh!
No evil spirit,
but it is I myself!

I am what I am, and
it is the being that I am
that drives me to the

dancing girls that
save my life and
soothe my heart.

What he said was true.
It was not a question
of right or wrong.

It was just the way he was,
though this knowledge may not
assuage the feeling of guilt.

There were deeper, more
compassionate ways of

understanding human
disposition and action
than blaming or praising.

LXXVIII

It was an old old story
since when he was young

and girls would gather
coal and pass through
the fields with baskets.

He was only twelve when
he was drawn to Krishna
with large brown eyes,

her face fair and smooth
and rich like milk. She was
sister of the boy Jawari.

Would that he could send a messenger
and call her to the gardens in the
evening, mellow as tree-ripe mangoes,
dropping with the scent of viburnum

and roses, or to the old English
park with a cannon and a tower,
where nightingales build their nests.

He would stare at her from the
much-trafficked hospital kitchen,

and it became known to everyone,
even to her in the Servants Quarters,

where she sat outside the courtyard,
what Sister John's boy was doing.

Then one day in the afternoon
queenly she walked down the
garden road between the rows

of sweet-peas growing tall on
stakes, marigolds, and lush red
poppies, pride of the gardener.

She came to their lattice door in the hot sun with
a dish of sweet rice and potato-cauliflower curry.

He stood paralyzed as she delivered
the food to the cook in the kitchen.
He stood there, saying nothing at all.

His staring at her was neither right nor wrong.
It was just the way he was drawn toward her.

He felt empty and incomplete without her,
as he would be drawn to others all his life.

There were times when the
question of right and wrong,
when a relationship evolved,

was like a man with a dagger
looming above him as he sat
lay in his cubicle in a brothel.

As when a woman was already committed,
as when the relation was inherently unequal,
as when the woman was among his students.

Whalen was a cheerleader, the
most attractive girl in his
introductory philosophy class.

She wore sandals with her faded
blue jeans and lovely blouses of
blue, red, purple, yellow, and white.

During games in the stadium he would
watch her get flipped in the air and the
band played and the crowd went Rah!

She would come early to class and they'd
make small-talk about odd gossipy things,

though he refrained from asking her about
her liaisons if any on the football team.

He did allow himself this.
Do you have a boyfriend?
Blaze asked. She said No.

How about Edgar? referring to a handsome,
strong, stocky young athlete in the class.
He had blonde curly hair and no tattoos.
He looks like the salt of the earth, said Blaze.

I'm trying my best, she said.
He's really sweet. A wrestler.
Crushed the guy from Lyons,
who was rated Number One.

He's preparing now for the State Championship
next year, and we're all telling him Go! Go! Go!

His dad's a coach at Wichita State and
his mom works at Northrock Baptist.

Blaze's relationship with Whalen
would have been wrong, though
erotic images fill his imagination

today in his old age
after fifteen years.

She comes to his door, and they
sit close together on the couch.

They talk softly and kiss. He
tells her how beautiful she is.

In the shower she soaps his
body, and he soaps hers.

Blaze Pascal learned from his mistakes.
He had paid the painful price for them
and had said, A door marked nevermore!
He knew those doors, those situations.

It was not an easy road,
being mindful of the
consequences of actions,

being stranded between Yes and No,
between love's draw and its dangers.

Love comes as a stranger who
beckons us on, as the song says.
But the other player is danger.

Blaze now understood the enormity
and the importance of sorting
these things out as his spiritual task.

Now he was thankful for this Creative City of
private detectives and dancing girls, catering

to the desert, the mountains, and the sea,
with a heart for empty, incomplete souls,
meaning dancers and dreamers such as he.

LXXIX

Blaze Pascal took the elevator up to the street,
said adios to the guard, walked down past the
taco stand and the new construction to Main.
He would return for his car after a short walk.

A man with twenty stuffed plastic bags in a
cart was gathering sundries on the sidewalk
alongside street-cleaner men with city vests.

The long line at an old theater was just beginning
to move for the Trickle Down Theory concert.

It still amazed him, he could not understand
it, the draw of this underground funky music.

Was it the illusion of community? A
stab at some alternate way of being?

Another theater was beaming
The Terminator, the old film
with Arnold Schwarzenegger.

A strong man went by partly talking,
partly singing to no one in particular.

The towers rose around him.
Square towers, round towers,
old towers, new towers,

fat towers, lean towers,
tall towers, short towers,

towers with a flash and a flare, dark straight
line towers against the glimmering city glow.

A voice kept whispering,
Go home, old man, to
the stillness of the slopes,
the silence of the sage.

Redeem yourself.
Dismantle, disembark.

Look away, look away,
look askance at the world.

New words are expected of you,
a new and oblique hermeneutics,
of things beautiful, true, and free.

Sing of the shoreline that is no more.
Yes, he recalled, Once I knew a shoreline
to which birds migrated in the spring.

Plovers and cormorants and quail,
sandpipers and sanderlings and willet,
flitted from tree to windblown tree
and sprinted in the sand and the sea.

I saw them build their nests in the
thickets and raise their families.

Then the land was sold, and
they cut the thickets and trees.

The birds no longer came in numbers
and the driftwood has been picked.

Here I walk sans destination
in the hope of consolation.

And void of resolution, save
to inscribe the word of peace,

the word that rises from the bottom of the sea,
the word that comes at the pond in the canyon,

the word in the stillness of the slopes,
the word in the silence of the sage.

LXXX

Through the valley of time he drives, and
the grip loosens of the half-moon night,

though You look Wonderful Tonight,
with its twangy guitar, still echoes, and
the shadows behind the veil still move.

Anbiguity, ignorance, and impermanence
hide the creativity of Sinatra and Torme,
private detectives and dancing girls,
musicians, movie stars, and Disneyland.

Even the moon is ambiguous,
turning the mist to
smoke rings beaming bright.

Cranes, blocked lanes, blinking arrows,
signaling new construction, take the place
of the starships, the glittering towers,

with their thousand squares of light, and
the restaurants, theaters, and cheap hotels.

Bleakly beautiful is the Khyber Pass
Bora Bora wilderness in the midnight

zone of warehouses, shopping malls,
Toyota parking lots, look-alike housing
developments, Chinese establishments.

We are gliding like a leaf in a stream
when suddenly now the traffic slows.

A family huddles,
officers scramble,
medics carry someone
on a stretcher.

We watch as we pass, and
we know our present madness,
and the price we pay in sadness.

Then Blaze Pascal cries,
Will you be my friend

when the powers and particles collide, and
the black holes and burning stars approach?

Will you stand with me
against the deaf soul
and the driven mind?

Will you still think of me,
will I still be in your eyes
and on your mind when

the winter rain comes
pouring down on my small
home near the desert,
the mountains, and the sea?

I see them always together,
the agitation and the disease.

The Zen group withdraws for silence.

LXXXI

He was in the hills now,
and he recalled the winds
that have blown upon him,

the winds of doctrine,
the winds of scarcity,
the winds of terror in a
swamp of hanging vines.

Did I hold my ground, like
the blind man had counseled,
the chaplain who advised
me in Sacramento, or

did I back down out of
existential necessity?

Did I reason with the minions,
the followers with forked tongues,
just as the chaplain had counseled,
or did I keep silent discreetly?

Did I face up to the woman
with the alligator eyes,
or give my power away?

The chaplain, a supervisor of chaplains at a
teaching hospital, a Fellow of the
National Association of Pastoral Counselors,

was soft-spoken, though direct, in
a noisy place, and he had a small
cramped office in a busy corridor.

His seminars were in the Chaplains Office,
where he taught fundamentalists and had
students of denominations high and low.

He used machines to read, and
I had to wait till he was finished.

Then he would turn and
my hour would begin.

Since the office was so porous,
the woman next door, quite young,
heard everything I said in private.

This did not bother him,
but I muffled my voice.

He looked down, as if he was asleep,
yet he was alert and knew my existentia.
Did he really understand my situation?

My wreckage was in process,
but he never did say retreat.

He was a rational man, and a fighter,
and he was teaching me how to fight,
and to face the question of being itself.

But I was never the purist, such as he.

I had reasoned with the minions and
had held my own against Alligator,
but she had her own personal agenda.

It was not the color of my skin:
It was the color of my soul.

She perceived me as a threat,
a mutant from an alien shore.

LXXXII

Writing by hand in the academic
libraries and sometimes in the
public library of Contemplation,

Blaze Pascal continued to set down his
thoughts and observations in free verse.

The days of Occupy were drawing to a close.
This we knew, though we survived the winter.

We met weekly to prepare initiatives
for the City Council of Contemplation.

I am a man of few words,
wrote Blaze Pascal, and
I labor over those I use,
and the meeting found me
stammering and stuttering.

Remorseful and without excuse, I
slumped through the alley, stopping
at rain puddles to view the universe,

and then at Platonic Coffee to
ask myself what went wrong.

Two rambunctious children from South India, silhouetted
in the whites of their mother's dark eyes, owned the cafe.

Journey Through the Past
by Neil Young cheered me.
Will I still be in your eyes
and on your mind?

I loved the version with guitars
and the harmonica,
the one used in Inherent Vice.

The Chamber had been full when
the five-member Council walked in.

We knew the Mayor, plump, smiling,
supportive of the sentiments at Ground.

The Hispanic gentleman with a scratched face and
a no-nonsense manner, professor of political science,
looked around knowingly above his reading glasses.

I found the Italian lawyer to be smart. A
slim man with a pointed nose, he seldom
spoke, but his few comments made sense.

The chairs were plush,
the floor polished, prepared
for the solemn hush.

The professionals with suits milling around,
who were they, what were they talking about,
before they disappeared behind closed doors?

The Mayor began with silence for the
victims of the shooting in Colorado.

Then I had stood in line when
Occupy made its statements.

The five men listened to my three minute saga
of forty years of watching and waiting, forty
years of preaching and teaching compassion.

How stunned we were in the 'seventies when
the mental health institutes were shut down
and the patients left to fend for themselves!

At last, I said, the voice
of the people is heard.

Not for power but
for principle.
Not for gold but
for the common good.

For food and shelter and medical care
for the homeless and the mentally ill.

Will the proud be scattered in the
imagination of their hearts, and the
hungry be filled with good things,
said I, quoting the verse in Luke.

It was dark now, the
trimmers had departed, the
last crows were settling in.

The breeze was in the cedars singing,
the half-moon was in the clouds flying.

Dead leaves chased after me in the night.
The eucalyptus made no sound at all.

LXXXIII

That weekend Blaze Pascal
again looked for Antonia,
listened to the songs, English
and Hispanic, and mused
near the ping-pong and pool.

The handsome Korean in preppy colors, his
face projecting poise, his pose confidence,
had been leaning against the cashier's desk,

and had approached Antonia quickly, rudely,
cutting out the rest of us when she appeared.

It won't be long, thought Blaze,
Antonia knows I'm waiting.

For all her bipolar problems,
Antonia is sensitive and
perceptive, and she is not
submissive to richer men.

This could have been the projection
of a needy mind, Blaze knew, but he
was inclined to think well of Antonia.

Now the material mind of the DJ was
playing Let the devil take tomorrow,
help me make it through the night,
while old man Blaze sought comfort

in philosophy and theology,
asking, Can fast or feast or
mammonic offering of the
young man make purchase
of the mystic passion?

Are not justice and mercy
and radical humility
the virtues love requires?

The secret of love is love itself,
the mystery of love a pure heart,
the story of love the mythic epic

of Kurukshetra and the call of duty,
or of the prince who leaves the palace

and witnesses for the first time
ignorance, disease, and death,

or of exodus and exile, or of
Galilee, death, and resurrection.

Such were old man Blaze's thoughts in
the hearing of shouts of victory and defeat
beside the tables of ping-pong and pool,

near the portraits of Marilyn Monroe,
Gary Cooper, Elizabeth Taylor,
and other famous Hollywood icons.

He watched for Antonia and the professional
Korean
to emerge from behind the veil of ignorance, and

listened to Never My Love,
Surfer Girl, Nat King Cole's
Rambling Rose, and the

Hispanic rhythms, to which he was seen
tapping his toes and rolling his shoulders.

LXXXIV

Over an hour had passed in the club crowded with men
in tailored clothes and some with tattoos on their arms,

and old man Blaze thought, It is
not all quiet on the western front.

But surely love is alive
and loose in the world.

It waits for us on the mountain
with its tenfold moral knowledge,
attended by clouds and thunder.

It abides with us
to break the bread
when it is evening
and the day far spent,

having walked with us,
the unknown stranger
on the dusty road,

to convey the consolation
that heals the wound
that bleeds in the night.

We asked ourselves,
Did not our hearts
burn within us?

Did we not breathe
deeply in and out?

Did we not breathe truth?
Did we not breathe love?

And such breathing is spirit for us,
said the Buddhist monk amazingly.

A tall older man with a saffron robe,
a strong voice, and a barrel chest,
at a conference at the seminary.

And from Abbey Road:
Aaaaaaahh!
Because the world is round
it turns me on.

Because the sky is blue
it makes me cry.

The Black Widow, sordid,
the color of deep shadows,
struck dangerously for her eggs

in a neglected room
upstairs in the church.

The lostness in each other of
Murad Begh and Suniti Pal,
the godlike surfers in the sea,
far away on the sea's horizon.

Murad the Moghul,
Suniti the Brahmin,
and all the others on the
transcendent crest of waves,

this is love, this is life,
and the children jumping
and screaming in the sea.

To be is to be related:
Thus the dharma is given.

This said a man at the
Brahmaputra on Gower.

What he said was true about
the nature of being and
the foundation of the world.

We begin relationships,
and so make promises
and incur obligations.

No naturalistic fallacy here.
Obligations simply arise.

No gulf between ought and is,
the latter being the ground
upon which the former grows.

And the owl that
hoots in the night,
it makes me brave
in the morning.

The hummingbird sitting
on a winter branch,
and now no more sitting
on the winter branch,

it moves me forward into the day.

Because so big the sky,
it lifts me high.

Because so deep the sea,
I have the courage to be.

And the word still comes
from the bush that burns
and is not consumed,

Take off your shoes,
this is holy ground,

the ground of being, the
foundation of the world.

LXXXV

O, and here come my
friends, the triplets,

wisdom, transcendence, critical thought.

I shall greet them
and ask them

to be my charioteer
in Kurukshetra,
the three in unison.

We come, they say, to guide you.

About my three friends:
Wisdom had emerged
from many a heartbreak,
bitter experience that is
now my inner resource.

It warns me, alerts me,
like a blinking yellow light.

Transcendence came naturally,
so shy I was among pretty girls,
and known to walk alone,

a homesick boy among
shooting stars and missionaries
along the Milky Way, and

anxious to climb up to the
mountaintop to be with them.

The philosophers taught me critical thought.
E.J. Lemmon had made it look easy, and it

was he who referred me
to Alonzo Church and
Chapter Zero in his book.

I studied the chapter with its footnotes,
all one hundred forty-nine of them.

They spoke of John Stuart Mill on connotation and denotation.
They spoke of Gottlob Frege on oblique referring to concepts.

I worked through most of the book
and began my career in philosophy.

Being young I was in a morass
about myself and my old beliefs.

New claims were in the air,
new theologies in the seminaries
and the open cultural marketplace.

But here was not a new claim to knowledge.

Here was a new way of thought,
which sharpened as I worked,

and with it grew a confidence
I had never experienced before,
a discovery on every page,

a new perspective for the new age,
a way of holding belief in abeyance.

To see clearly,
to feel stronger,
it was a miracle.

I needed these friends of old,
because the dragon jealousy,
vicious he, had degraded me,
breathing fear, sowing suspicion.

Then it happened that
the demigod desire,

no friend of the triplets,
but an opposing force,
asserted itself
ironically in my defense.

Now there emerged within me
power and control at once.

I could not say Peace! and
command the waves Be still!

Yet I would not languish under
the portrait of Gary Cooper
beside the ping-pong and pool.

LXXXVI

Be brave, my heart, said I, on the street
of Brother can you spare some change.

The blue moon sees you
stand without love,
dreamless and alone,

as it sees this old woman
with the cart of bulging bags,
empty bottles and cans,
and blankets for the night,

and the men in her situation
near the taco stand
under the light at the corner.

Wicked it would be
to go back inside, to
kiss without meaning,
caress without feeling.

Let no echo of dance
or lure of romance
sway this just resolve.

No sooner had I said this that
nimble women and Viking men,

rebels with tattoos, Mohawks,
and Gothic silver,
sauntered down the street.

One woman looked flirtingly
up at the uncouth guard with

camouflage pants, heavy
army boots, and holstered gun,

asking, What happens here? her face
beaming brightly through her rings.

We listened to the drama of
the man explaining the place
in broken English and
untamed Salvadoran accent.

Then I walked away.

LXXXVII

One week later sitting in a
downtown restaurant in the

Creative City of Angels, Blaze
wrote this on his scratch paper.

I saw police on horses and
electrified vehicles chat
leisurely on a street corner.

Forty Hispanic youth
bicycled on Wilshire Boulevard,
slowing down the rush hour.

What power to command
the city this way!
Freedom like no other!

Freedom too of the storefront
church on Eighth near Vermont
to blare out anthropomorphisms
about the Battle of Armageddon

and the apocalypse of Babylon,
mother of all harlots and abominations,
source of the great tribulation,

sitting on a monster beast
with seven heads and ten horns,
arrayed in purple and scarlet

and jewels and pearls, holding a
cup of wine from her fornications
with the many heads of nations.

Behold I stand at the door and knock:
Those who hear me and open the door,
I will come in and sup with them.

I entered and listened,
declining the chair,
and opting to stand.

The man and woman deacons
at the back looked at me
with questions in their hearts,

while women and men,
youth and children,
lifted their hands high,

saying, Hallelujah! Hallelujah!
Salvation belongs to our God!

as the man in the front spoke
loudly into the microphone and
the organ played an affirming
Gospel tune in the background.

I have seen your tribulation and your poverty
and the slander to which you are subjected.

Fallen, fallen is Babylon the
dwelling place of foul spirits!

Fallen, fallen is Babylon,
making the nations to drink
the wine of her fornication!

Babylon fallen,
fallen, fallen!

Alas for the great city,
clothed in fine linen,

in purple and scarlet,
bedecked with gold,
jewels, and pearls:

No more shall be heard in it
the sound of music and dancing,
or of craft and the millstone,

or the joyful voices of
groom and bridegroom.

No more to be seen the
light of the street lamp.

Portents in earth and sky we see.
A Beast rising out of the sea
with ten horns and seven heads.

Like a leopard is he with
bear's feet and lion's mouth,

instrument of Babylon,
speaking blasphemies and lies.

The dragon Satan, thrown
down to the earth from heaven,
gives its authority to the Beast,

whose power is spreading
as far as the eye can see.

People are saying, Who
is like the Beast, and
who can fight against it?

It detains us,
it deports us.

We hear talk about the wall.
The wall, the wall, the wall.

Woe to those who separate families and
bring heartbreak upon brothers and sisters!

Woe to those who separate
husbands and wives,
mothers and daughters,
fathers and sons!

Woe to those who turn away
seekers of asylum at the border!

Blessed are they who take shelter
under the wings of Holy Spirit,

whose robes are washed in the blood of
the Lamb that was slain and has conquered!

Hallelujah! Hallelujah!
Salvation belongs to
our God and to the Lamb!

LXXXVIII

Old man Blaze ruminated in MacArthur Park
on the things he had just heard in the church.
It was now evening and the day was far spent.

He understood the fear
for themselves and their
families, some of whom

perhaps undocumented, of
detention and deportation.

He was an immigrant himself.
He had known the fear himself.

His heart went out also to the Muslim
refugees being detained at the airports.

He understood the need for
the kingdom of anxiety to
become the higher kingdom
of truth and consolation.

He himself straddled the
kingdom of anxiety and the
higher kingdom of truth.

Human overpopulation, he knew,
is the root cause of Babylon, which
extends as far as the eye can see.

He had heard moralistic explanations:
They did not seem to go deep enough.
Greed was not the cause but the result.

Armageddon is the name of our age,
the age of terror and surveillance, the

age of idolatry and worldedness,
age of fragmentation and identity,
like the man from Geneva had said,

the de-wilding of the lands and waters, and
the extinction of species in untold numbers.

The human trafficking of women and children
and the exploitation of animals for profit,
the smuggling of chimps and the poaching of
elephants, rhinos, apes, tigers, snow leopards.

The abandonment of domestic animals
especially on holidays, he heard some say.

He watched the gulls that came close up to him,
the soccer games of the youth on the green, and
the scattering of homeless persons everywhere.

He strolled among the sellers on the crowded streets
of fruits and flowers and phones and soaps and sprays,
remembering the Tanka Wali Basti in Ferozepore and
Chandni Chowk in Old Delhi, near the Red Fort there.

He searched for an answer, but no answer came,
except that of shining the light in the darkness:

Practicing renunciation, simplicity, restraint.

Restraint in the dining hall,
restraint in the marketplace,
restraint in the somber hours.

Practicing goodness,
pursuing enlightenment,
teaching compassion
and the quest for truth.

Be still and behold the great western star,
and the twinkle of light in the purple dusk.

Be silent, hear the wind in cedars,
the mystic call in unmystic times.

On the mountain,
hear the call,
the mystic call!

In the sea,
hear the call,
the mystic call!

On the rock,
hear the call,
the mystic call!

Open the windows of the mind to
art and literature and philosophy.

Teach, learn, dialogue.
Teach, learn, dialogue.

This will bring to the soul its consolation,
as Boethius told from his imprisonment
by the Ostrogoth Theodoric long long ago.

That night Blaze Pascal tipped
the dancing girls well at Club
Zero for their children and families
here and south of the border.

Santiago, Guadalupe, Huatulco Bay.

They gave the old man kisses
and quickly looked away.

This he kept to himself,
having no intimate friends,
no one he drew close to.

His friends could be moralistic.
Some stressed inner cleanliness,
others were obsessive activists,
still others conspiracy theorists.

One had a special interest in Blaze,
and he paid special attention to her.

She was pretty and petite,
dressed in flowing robes, and
had long white curly hair.

She levitated one yard above the
ground after her daily chapel routine.

She floated smoothly, like a friendly
ghost, quite unaware of the sacred

light she beamed effulgently upon each
person she stopped for, to
exchange a greeting or just to smile upon.

From one friend Blaze heard a martial
voice in defense of her pious practices.

It was a survival thing,
the stance itself, a fortress,
which meant stay away.

Another looked down contemptuously
on contemporaneity in art and music.

Few advocated philosophical
and literary enlightenment or

the vigorous cultivation of an
open mind in one's golden age.

LXXXIX

Julianne's stylings were versatile,
and had blended immersively
with heart, mind, and soul,

at the Private Eye Piano Bar
on Sunset west of Cahuenga,

a plush upscale place with its own parking lot,
shared with big highrise apartments at the back.

Her piano chords were resonant, like
the chimes of Contemplation that
come from the verandahs of the rich,

and her voice lilting and supple,
like the singing style of Joanie
Sommers, who had sung Pepsi's

For Those Who Think Young and
hits like Johnny Get Angry and
the song Blaze loved, One Boy.

She wore handsome sweatsuits,
gray and black, in the winter,

and Punjabi colorful sylvar and
kamiz outfits and blue-green
flowing skirts in the summer.

Blaze Pascal had sat rapt hearing
songs like As Time Goes By,
Someone to Watch Over Me,
New York State of Mind, and

Under the Boardwalk, in which
the whole club joined in the chorus.

And she had noticed him sitting nearby week by
week, watching, listening, sending in requests.

Lean and tall, she was this side of forty with
light brown hair falling straight down.
He could see strands of gray at the fringes.

On one occasion, she stood up for her break
and walked to his table to introduce herself.

That evening she was dressed like a monk,
wearing a loose-fitting bright yellow saffron
shirt that came down to her knees, and
loose-fitting saffron pants the deep red of fire.

He stood up for her and looked closely into
her hazel eyes and she into his green eyes.

They were face to face trying
to gauge one another, and he
invited her to sit down with him.

I am Blaze Pascal, he said, and told her
how attracted he was to her voice
and how she could woo the world with it.

You are originally from India,
she said this as a question, and what
are you doing here in America?

He could feel both gravity and discipline,
long cultivated over the years,
draw them together and hold them apart.

It was the tension he had come to
know between power and control.

My country of origin is India, he said, and
my background is philosophy and religion.

How do you practice your philosophy and religion?
She was sensing something, perhaps a mild kinship.

I am retired from teaching philosophy
and being a philosophical sort of pastor.

I spent a year in India, she
said, in two ashrams there,

one in Santiniketan and one
in the community inspired by
Aurobindo in Pondicherry.

What drew you to those places especially?
His curiosity and surprise had gotten deeper.

It's a long story, she said. I was influenced
by Eastern philosophy when in college at
Berkeley, especially by Rabindranath Tagore's

poetry about the unity of humanity, where the
mind is without fear, where knowledge is free,

where the world is not broken
up into fragments by domestic
walls, as he himself phrased it.

I'm still in awe of his rapturous poems, in
which on the seashore of endless worlds,
pearl fishers may dive for pearls, merchants

may sail on their ships, but children
gather pebbles and scatter them again.

She said this expressively,
almost as if it was song.

Indeed, Blaze recalled,
for Tagore it was a song,

just as for Blaze his own verses
were often intended as songs.

She gestured the gathering and the scattering of
the pebbles by the children widely with her arms.

She started telling Blaze P about how she lived in a
mud hut and took walks in the grove of neem and pipal
and among the herds of deer playing in the forest preserve,

and had problems with Santiniketan being
built up by Western architecture catering
to the university and modernity in general,

but she stood up and hastened back to the piano.

He said as she was walking away that he would
like to hear her thoughts about Aurobindo also.

Next time, she said, I'll share his
poetic retelling of the Mahabharata
love story of Satyavan and Savitri.

XC

Blaze Pascal was undone by the range and depth
of her thoughtfulness and frame of reference,
and the maturity of her spiritual and poetic sensibility,

which got expressed so naturally in the way she sang too,
and he would look for a chance to sit with her again. But

it was later in the month that
she was not there on Friday.

Instead he heard Lacienfuegos Jazz at
the Private Eye render the old songs
with a postmodern post-Ipanema hum,

though Antonia Carlos Jobim
could still be heard, and
he knew again how quiet nights
of quiet stars drive the world.

No noisy gongs or clanging cymbals here,
no hypocrisy, love still visible everywhere.

Certainty had passed away.
Information had ceased:

Devices rendered useless
At the tables, at the bar,

when the saxophone played
and the base strummed and
the drum combined with the
electronic dissonant sound.

The desert persuades the ocean wind,
and no one understands the mystery.

The tall tan girl,
young and lovely,
still walks in Ipanema,

and all the people
go Ahhhhhhhhhh!

Was it Julianne?
Was it Julianne?

Dead souls rise
to dance the bossanova,

the mythic chakra of
life and death,
known as samsara.

The waves part and let them through
toward their nirvana, their
liberation from the endless wheel,

and all the people go Ahhhhhhhhhh!

Then the mist rolls
in from the sea

to sever the moon
and darken the world.

The equivocal age
seeks its resolution,
and the roving heart
its benediction,

in the soul's dark night.

See the boy wind up
to the mountaintop,
the moon streaking
through the deodars.

Higher and higher
he climbs alone to
hear the mystic
missionaries sing.

Now the mist rises
from the ravines,
bringing a soft rain,
to overtake him.

The moon is no more,
the snows he cannot see
nor the lights in the plains

from outside the church,
near the old cemetery.

In the mist,
in the rain,

he hears the call,
the mystic call.

XCI

The Private Eye had filled up nicely
since old man Blaze had entered.

The people were middle aged and older, here to
listen to The First Time Ever I Saw Your Face
and other favorite standards of their generation.

Some younger men were
there, just looking around.

Blaze Pascal finished his orange juice.
The small wine glass with lots of ice
cost him over nineteen dollars, not

counting the tip for Rob, the bartender,
a young George Clooney look-alike.

He said that Julianne plays at other clubs too.
The Beach Bar, not far from Santa Monica beach,
caters to a mixed crowd of rich surfer wannabes,
young college couples, and off-the-street hippies.

He said this while mixing drinks for customers,
using the cash register, and running into
the other bartenders,waiters, and waitresses.

Blaze had been at the Beach Bar years ago
and knew it as a loud beer joint on Fridays
with rock and roll groups providing the music.

He assumed she played there on weekdays.

She sings north of here too,
Rob said, but wasn't quite sure,
at the Reef, an exclusive joint

known for the movie stars and other VIPs
in the industry that drop in occasionally.

You might not like the snooty culture of
the place with its valet parking, Rob said,

and its dress codes even for the waitresses and
waiters, dressed up to here, signaling his neck.

Julianne should be back in three months,
which is the usual length of their break.

It was busy at the counter, but
when Rob had a minute Blaze
asked him if he was in college.

I'm taking classes at a culinary school here
in Hollywood with Rosemary, my girlfriend.

We both hope to graduate
in a year and look for work,
preferably here in California,

but the competition for a
decent wage is rough here.

Blaze wished Rob well and stepped out,
driving east on Sunset for the One-O-One.

He would wait for Julianne's return.
He would drop in regularly and watch the
web for the schedule of Private Eye.

His soul filled with moon and music as he
drove the freeway past the sparkling skyline
and past big corporate buildings beyond,

His soul filled with moon and music as he
drove the freeway past the sparkling skyline
and past big corporate buildings beyond,

some with tall evergreens, making them
attractive with their lights partly hidden.

There was no getting away from Julianne
or Lacienfuegos Jazz at the Private Eye,

and the radio too was playing a funk dance
track, to which he now was strangely glued.

Mostly an electronic drumbeat
interrupted by quick unintelligible
ethereal sounds, signals from
an alien galaxy light years away.

The DJ called himself the British
Invasion and had an English accent.

When you stop the moon stops.
It loves you, you love it back.

It was the dead of night.
Blaze's train had stopped at
the small empty station.

Godse the fundamentalist was
hanged here in Kurukshetra,
in accordance with the law.

Not like the man in the story
told by Alonzo Church about
a bridge, a gallows, and
a law pertaining to them.

Persons swearing falsely, when asked,
Why do you choose to cross the bridge?
must be hanged according to the law.

Those who swore truthfully
may be allowed to cross.

One man comes to the bridge and swears,
I go to be hanged on yonder gallows.

Church asks us to show that in
this case the law cannot be obeyed.

Godse came to the bridge and swore,
I go to say my evening prayers.

He would later push through the crowd,
pay his obeisance, and fire three times
upon Satyagraha, the face of truth itself.

The full moon was rising now upon
the epic battlefield and the platform.

A solitary soul went by,
dark against the moon,
chanting garm chai, garm chai.
Which means hot tea, hot tea.

XCII

The clouds cloaked the moon into Batman.
Brake lights flared, the traffic came to a stop.

A gaunt spry young man carrying
a can was crossing the freeway.

The medallion on his vest and the
whites of his eyes pierced the night.

He smiled and gestured thanks into the glare,
as if to say, Don't worry 'bout me, I'll be alright.

Have you, Blaze Pascal, ever run
out of gas in the dead of night?

Not in the dead of night, no, but yes,
we were overtaken by the dark between
Upper and Lower Tahquamenon Falls
in the Hiawatha National Forest.

Ruled by roots,
lashed by limbs,
we hiked on,

thankful for the moon in the river.

Now in the parking lot a bird shrieks close by.
Hold still, says Blaze Pascal, in the late watch.
What arrow flies in the heart of darkness?
What worm creeps in the bowels of the night?

Ponder, chaplain, before you sleep,
your own finitude among
the sirens of perpetual perishing.

Muse, monk, on the cursedness
of the world seized unto itself.

Brood, philosopher, on the courage to be
as the courage to be known for who you are.

Be known, Blaze Pascal, then bide your
time for the executioner, who will come
for you as surely as he came for Boethius.

XCIII

Look! In the shrub
the bees are buzzing!

In the pool
the children are playing!

In the rocks
the snake is slinking!

Blaze Pascal was thin, with
classic features, and known
to look unshaven at times.

His color was brown, his eyes green,
and his speech was slow, deliberate.

A man of good humor, an exact
copy of his grandmother, he said.

Again he heard a word from
the wilderness and the river,

and the word reasserted
what it had taught before,
the mysticism of the hollow wind.

Blaze was impatient and nervous about
the return of Julianne to Private Eye,
which he expected to be in three weeks,
and the word of the hollow wind was,

Do not be anxious in
the interval between
the now and the not-yet.

Practice the positive yoga of action,
the writing of your verses day by day,
the cultivation of friendship with all.

Also the negative yoga of inaction,
restraint, renunciation, and solitude.

Blaze thought of his verses
to be like a peace sign he
held up on a busy street
during rush hour traffic.

Some honk affirmingly, he wrote.
Many are not yet ready for peace.

Perhaps at an easier time, when
the children are not home alone,
and other jobs are available, and
prices are within reach, we will

work toward reconciliation and
moderation, a middle ground.

Meanwhile the students throw
away their paper cups, their
exquisite Starbucks paper cups.

They fall in love, they
seduce one another,

many in turmoil,
searching for direction

or change of direction.

They, like the best of us,
suppress the large questions

about the mysticism of life,
the meaning of these days.

Truth is not taught in
the sense of wisdom.

Beauty is relegated to small
print, if it is mentioned at all.

The human empire grows,
the wilderness shrinks,
species go extinct, and
what prevails is unconcern.

On the beach
the birds are running!

High in the sky
the eagles are flying!

In the sea
the dolphins are leaping!

Forgive my epistemology, but
ours is not propositional knowing.

It is a true knowing in the
I-Thou land of unknowing,

the walk on the forest floor, the
inspiration of the hollow wind,
the stopping at the vibrant pond.

In the pines
the wind is singing!

In the stream
the water is gushing!

In the cafe
Holger and Julio
are laughing!

XCIV

Come with me
to the sea of love

and the shipwrecked thrones
on the ocean floor.

Behold the souls who
were left for dead,

who rose to love
and laugh again.

I see them at
Point Conception
rising from the sea.

'Mid violence they
sheltered others, and
held out for peace.

Betrayed they still said,
Let us love one another.

They organized and spoke

out in the name of truth.
Oppressed, degraded, they
marched for their freedom.

Blind they counseled
floundering souls.

I was one who rose again and
laughed, learned, and loved again,

inspired by teachers of
the mysticism of truth
to the modern morass.

I knew on the trains that took me away,
looking out on the fields of brown, on the
revolution of bullocks in vicious circles, on
the patience of vultures on naked limbs,

that the sameness would be
only the moon coming along.

Left in cold and snowy places
I grew to love my friends.

Clive Agnome was the fiery one,
a fearsome tiger among the boys.

He bashed me across the jaw in the crowd.
People pulled me away and no fight ensued.
He was bigger than me and afraid of no one.

But he was my companion
on the forest trails.

Once in the monsoon rain

he'd turn back to
pull leaches off my shoes.

Freyja, the celestial one,
Norse goddess, the most
beautiful girl in the world,

waited for me in the abandoned cabin,
brightened by pines and pine-needles.

I hiked from across
the deep ravine,
jumped on boulders
crossing the stream,

for the sweetness of her kisses
and the softness of her breasts.

I loved her letters
in blue envelopes.

Arthur Pocock, the amiable one,
led me on the winding dirt path
to the lovely valley of the Dun,

hoping we would find the peanut-walla
with raw brown sugar and pastries as well.

We were one in our difference
from the boys of that school,

he with his physical differences,
I with my ethnic background.

Terrence was the unfortunate one.
He was handsome and athletic, but
was not the brightest of the boys.

Withdrawn, submissive, he was afraid
to compete against the dominant ones.
His goal? Survival in a violent world.

During the summer vacation,
treated badly by his mother,
he came for shade to our house
in the grueling heat of the plains.

O Terrence, did you succeed in
leaving the country after all?
Where are you now, sweet friend?

XCV

Yes, I was one who rose again
to laugh, learn, and love again.

I ran from Hanuman langurs in the forest,
collected and studied maidenhair ferns
and stag beetles for Mr. O. B. Perkins.

Miss Lawie's piano and often her cello,
coming from upstairs as I lay sleeping,

galloped like a stallion across
the mountains triumphantly.

Then when the piano and cello were done,
and the loud chorus of crickets had ceased,
the village flute arose in the night, as if

from an ancient mountain village
set among rice paddies, which
would erode in the monsoons

and again be rebuilt, and sown
in the fall with wheat and barley.

I learned it came from the Servants Quarters
outside the very dorm in which I lay sleeping.

It was high but not shrill.
Its aim was not to conquer,

like the horns and conches
of the battlefield Kurukshetra,
preparing the men for battle,

or the angry virulent piano
just played by Miss Lawie.

The flute expressed
the joy and peace of
being with one's family
when the day is done.

XCVI

The word came to me, the word
of holy spirit and human spirit,

It is time. Let us visit
the land of the dead.

There you shall understand
the meaning of life, that it
has a beginning and an end.

And you, Blaze Pascal, your
life is near the end,
your powers are diminished.

Soon you will no longer
visit the Creative City
of Hollywood and Vine,

of gods and goddesses,
of rising and falling,
of falling and rising, or

go down to the sea to
challenge the waves
or walk in the sand,

hear the children play,
and watch the surfers
fly in the sky when
the waves break high.

Thus it was that I found myself in
the Valley of the Skull, walking
for miles and seeing no living thing.

The isolation was all in all.
The emptiness, the silence.

No snake or scorpion or spider.
No cactus or pinion on the slopes.

I heard no spring or stream in the
cracks and gullies among the rocks.

And as I walked I remembered
that my father's bones were here,

though not the stories of his travels,
which belong to the land of the living,
to be told here on these very pages.

His arrivals and departures, his tales about the
magnificent city of the Empire State Building,

the skyscrapers with elevators
rising to a hundred floors, and

places you could buy both
safety pins and battleships.

And the famous churches
with their great preachers:

George Buttrick's books were
lying in my father's small library.

Norman Vincent Peale, whose book
on the power of positive thinking
was a New York Times bestseller.

Harry Emerson Fosdick
of the Riverside Church,
close to Columbia University
and Teachers College and

Union Theological Seminary,
where my father did his doctorate.

The staggering ideas of Reinhold Niebuhr
on the self and the dramas of history, and

on the children of light, who believe in reason,
and the children of darkness, despairing of reason,

on the paradoxes that inhere
in the very heart of faith,
the contradictions persisting

in both success and failure,
in both war and peace,
in both religion and reason.

Effervescent was my
father about them all.

Niebuhr's The Nature and destiny of Man and
Lewis Mumford's Technics and Civilization

were both right there in the cabinet too.
I browsed in them, when I was out of my
Captain Marvels and Zane Grey westerns,
but could not make much sense of them.

XCVII

Fragmentation,
said the man from Geneva.
Identity,
said the man from Geneva.

My father came back home
to a ruined marriage and a
country in tsunamic change.

The Partition was underway.
The Punjab was engulfed in
violence the scale of which
the world had never seen.

The rich Hindus in Lahore seem to
have known it was coming and had
fled the beautiful historic metropolis,
leaving behind all their belongings.

But the religious violence,
the mobs, the looting,
the raping, the burning,

between the Muslims
on the one side
and the Hindus and Sikhs
on the other side,

it was truly terrifying.

And happening all over the Punjab.
Ambushed trains of refugees coming
into the stations with dead bodies.

There was no one to stop the lunacy.
The British troops were leaving
on their humongous military ships.

The Indian army was itself divided,
the men anxious about their families.

In the end the mass migration
numbered fifteen million.
Nearly two million were dead.

Fragmentation,
said the man from Geneva.
Identity,
said the man from Geneva.

And Gandhi was fasting.
Many deserted him.
India was rejoicing on
its Independence Day.

Many would find it sad,
the defeat of Satyagraha
by the mobs on the streets,
the shouting of slogans.

I hear them now,
the slogans of identity.

They echo in my soul,
the shouts of fragmentation.

The defeat of Satyagraha by
the worlded idolatrous mind.

The defeat of spirit by
existential necessity.

XCVIII

Between Lahore and Ferozepore is a big
river, frightening for a small boy of nine.

I had gone across the bridge on
the train with my beloved aunt to
visit my other aunties and cousins,

and had absorbed the hollow
vibrations, fateful, ominous, the
metal bars whizzing by in a blur.

I had watched the river far
below, its midnight glow,
its dark waters of death,

the waters of fragmentation,
not the waters of healing.

It was a year before the Partition.

After the Partition my Uncle Priti
brought my mother back to India in
his shiny new car, whose polished
leather seats smelled nice and fresh.

No one told me the significance
of my mother's return till later.

Of my father's brothers and sisters,
Uncle Priti, the adventuresome one,
was perhaps the most bodacious
and wily, though he was quite short.

He left his wife and family in Lahore
and disappeared some place overseas.

He made appearances now and then,
looking rich, but was still secretive.

There were rumors aplenty.
Some said that he had indeed
become rich, trading in pearls,
diamonds, and sapphires, and

had acquired dual citizenship
of both England and Pakistan.

Some said that he had gone
underground and joined the
pirates of the Persian Gulf,

delivering arms to the Saudis
and to the other principalities.

Others said that he was in prison
and never to be heard from again,
but time proved them very wrong.

My father remained a divided man,
but he was quiet about his troubles.

We lived, all of us, ambivalently,
between faith and unavowed doubt,
between trust and suppressed fear,
between hope and alienation.

XCIX

Prince's bones were scattered
here in the Valley of the Skull.

We had grown close,
the sheep dog and I.

He came with us from the Punjab to Delhi,
where my father had acquired a churchy job.

I took Prince for long walks and
carried him across street crossings.
I still feel his warm body in my arms.

I feel Connaught Place
itself behind me and
around me as I walk,

just as the valley of dry
bones surrounds me
and stretches before me.

But I was a mere youth then, and
it was the eve of my own departure.

The worlds were colliding,
East and West, old and new.

I was swept up in the collision
and unaware how deep my love.

How deep my love,
how deep my love,

I was unaware
how deep my love.

How blinded I was as a youth!
Blinded about the world within,
blinded by the world without.

Blinded about how to think.
Blinded even about myself.

Powerful emotions within,
stresses, pressures without.

My religion was a mere fundamentalism
expressing itself crudely on the streets.

I did not know to hold in abeyance
what I should think, what I should do.

As Prince and I walked
around Connaught Place,
past banks and restaurants,

cinemas, textile shops, and
The Statesman newspaper,

I was unaware of
how deep my love.

And as we walked side by side
past taxi and rickshaw stands,
betel nut and cigarette stalls,

corporate offices,
street corner beggars,

samosa and chola wallas,
the Hindustan Times,

night clubs featuring
groups from Goa,
bicycle and auto places,

where I saw the new 1956 Thunderbird,
sleek, shiny, and beautiful, and stopped
to gaze and prophesy that later models
would be big and mean and clunky,

my insides were on fire for Pan American
waiting to fly me into the sky,

and for the President Cleveland in Hong Kong
waiting to sail me on the sea.

It made me dumb to
raise the question of
Prince's future care.

C

O human soul,
can these bones live?

I gave no answer.

Prophesy to these bones
and to the four winds.

I prophesied as I was told.

No sound came of wind
or of the rattling of bones.

No coming together of
neck bone to the shoulder bone,
knee bone to the thigh bone.

The isolation was all in all.
The emptiness, the silence.

I wondered about Terrence,
whether he was still alive,
and about Arthur Pocock.

*Arthur, Arthur, are you alive, or
are your bones scattered here?*

*Do you remember, my friend,
how we walked on Saturdays
on dirt paths outside the school,*

*and came once upon the blue
highway winding steeply
down down down to the
beautiful valley of the Dun,*

*and also upon the Halfway Bazaar,
where we looked for the peanut
walla who had brown sugar and
pastries, and could not find him?*

We made it back that time,
didn't we, for roll call at 5?

Arthur was a mutant, as was I,
in the pugilistic culture of the
Anglo-Indian school, a culture
whose bones I knew were here.

He had odd feet and an awkward walk
and was slightly effeminate in his talk.

I had been transferred from an American school across
the ravine, and my difference was marked from the start.

I too had a different way of talking, and
there were others like us, misfits, and
between us all was an understanding,
secret, unspoken, consoling us privately.
I have friends now at the infirmary.

CI

Some of the disabled smile kindly.
Some sit still or recline in silence.
Some lament loudly for attention.

I visit them all as volunteer chaplain
in private rooms and common spaces.

Board games and stretching groups are often
in progress. I stop by to support the therapist
who's leading them and to greet my friends.

They are happy and laugh when I join them.

I started chaplaining by doing
religious group therapy, but
I have not done that for years.

Fundamentalists, religious and medical,
have disturbed and confused me here.

A ninety year old woman,
bandaged across her eyes,
was kept in her room,

visited only by her staff
and religious friends.

She lay and heard Mozart
and Beethoven all day long.

It was unusual to see her one day sitting
in Central Space, near the nurses' station.

It was the intersection for all wheel chair,
staff, and visitor traffic at the infirmary.

I sat down and talked with her,
asking her about how she liked
sitting here in this location. Yes,
she said, in her weakened voice.

In this space, while she
could not see, she could
hear the world stop and go.

She could hear Gospel songs in a distant room,
hear about the brightness of the evening star
and about a resident's schizophrenic daughter,

and exchange a word perhaps with visitors,
other residents, their family members, staff.

Healing was in the hearing.
Healing was in the intercourse.
Healing was in the touching

and being touched, and even
being bumped into by the crowd
of wheel chairs, nurses, therapists,
staff, and volunteers there to help.

Central Space was a Platonic Point, a
place of knowing and grasping truth,

where the mind is active and
experience expands exponentially,
yes, even at ninety years of age.

In a letter I wrote I said so
then and there to her doctor.

It gladdened my heart, I explained, to
see Mary sitting outside and listening to,
interacting with, the world around her.

How critical, this, for her mental health.
Let us do this more often, I urged.

I gave the letter to the charge nurse,
asking that it be placed in her chart.

Nothing came of it. The
letter did not reach the doctor.

Some asked, Why did you not
consult her care-giver friends?

But I had talked with them,
and they had said simply,
No, Mary is light-sensitive.

CII

All my friends are old like me,
and they too are diminishing.

We will all go down in
the age of surveillance.

Our trains will pull away
imperceptibly
to the Valley of the Skull.

We know we will leave, and
we have prepared our hearts.

But before we leave,
will we find our way out
of our room of opinion
and our world of belief?

Some are rigid in their opinions,
some comfortable in their beliefs,
and unable to see any reason to
unlearn what they have learned.

Some are quite able to think
but are unwilling to change
because they too are content,

or busy caring for their bowels
or broken limbs, waiting for
their physical therapy, or
expecting a visit from family.

Few are already at Platonic Point
and skeptical about the world
and about what's coming down.

Still reaching for the light they
welcome their places at the
edge, precipices overhung by

an ancient short-needle pine
on a big rock beside the sea,

where they see not only
the world behind them,

but the vast conceptual sea
of consolation in front of them,

the sea of courage, hope,
love, justice, the virtues,

the ocean of being,

forms that mystics
east and west wear
when they enter
the soul's dark night.

Be still, and let the dark come upon you,
which shall be the darkness of the soul.

There at the edge we are healed,
our horizons are liberated from
our small rooms of contentment.

CIII

We spoke at the spring equinox
about justice with Jivaka Johns,
a retired professor of ethics.

I was glad so many joined us.
Thirty or forty were present.

The tension between the form
and the world engaged us, the

tension between justice the idea
and the stories of its embodiment
or denial in the dramas of history.

Yes, said George Andrews,
retired philosopher, to Jivaka,

your emphasis upon narrative
rather than theory promises
to lead us to authenticity
and is welcome in my heart:

I have seen so many theories
get bogged down in argument.

He spoke with an intense, passionate voice, though
it wavered slightly, being heard by so many intently.

People looked up to him because he
urged the avoidance of argumentation.

Simone Peterson spoke out about
her deceased husband Jacob,
who raised money for the lawyers
who defended the Sanctuary workers.

James Greenwood, a frail retired church leader, was quiet, I
observed, and I wondered what he thought and how he felt.
John Hastings, another retired pastor, was unusually silent.

Did they feel grateful?
Did they feel enlightened?
Did they feel liberated?

They were receptive certainly.

Daniel Davenport, a retired attorney,
said that the quest for justice
is really the quest for reconciliation.

Feminists then introduced right
relationship as germane to justice.

Right relationship between women
and men became a central example.

We went back to our homes with
fresh thoughts on justice and
the foundations of the moral life,

thoughts that seemed to buzz
and leap and zoom and loom
and fly away like bees.

Before our trains depart, we shall join,
some of us, Bertrand Russell's
A Free Man's Worship, having received
the light, the knowledge, the lofty
thoughts that ennobled our little day.

CIV

As philosopher I had buried
religion but had exhumed it,

and what a stunning surprise it was,
dressed in its brand new hermeneutic!

I had lost my way years ago,
experimenting with the academic
life of teaching philosophy,

but grew frustrated with the system
and its rules and the mediocrity
that reigned in the department,

and had decided to give my
original road a second chance.

And I, the new philosophical
pastor and aspiring theologian,

stumbled and fell,
and rose again,
a stronger man.

Beauty ingresses into the soul,
like the ocean into the shore.
Then know that it withdraws.

Truth comes to us as we walk.
Its river rises in our hearts.
Then know that it withdraws.

Half-truths go by at
downhill skateboard speed.

Among the philosophers in the city
I had given himself to the questions.

How, I asked, to move
beyond mere abstraction?

Don't sink too deep, they said,
and pointed always to Willard,

Willard Van Orman Quine.
Willard Van Orman Quine.

Follow the lead, they said,
of Willard Van Orman Quine.

I was lonely among them and knew
I was missing something essential.

The time had come to
reconcile with my past.

I searched for my road for three
years among the churches, and
found buried among their treasures
the Reverend William T. Scott,

a retiring middle-aged man,
pastor of the Briarcliff Church,

hidden behind pines and maples,
dogwood and tulip trees, and
looking out upon rhododendrons.

CV

The person of heaven unknowingly
gave to the person of dust a prayer.

Blaze was nothing less than astonished
when William T proved, in a certain sense
of prove, using well-chosen poetic words,
not without the light touch of humor about

Clark Kent and Lois Lane,
and good cops and bad cops,

the nonlinear mystical truth of religion,

to bind the arms of justice,
to loose the arms of mercy,

to sing for ignorant
bishops and pastors,
unfaithful to the end,

bought out for gold,
bought for small change,

and to use Charles Pegay's long
prayers to say to The Waste Land
how the world really ends,

not with a bang, not with a whimper,
but with a doxology, an Amen, and a
fleet of prayers with a pointed prow.

William T reawakened in me
the controversy of theology.

He himself was a man of prayer.
His way of being in the world
was prayer, not submergence.

Prayer was the way he reached outward,
prayer was the way he reached inward.

Prayer was the way he reached upward,
prayer was the way he reached downward.

Blaze tried for a closer knowledge.
Others tried for a closer knowledge.

It was no use. William
T was just William T.

He used who he was,
he used what he was,

to give himself and others
an aesthetic, sacred space.

All this brought him trouble. The
church's activists were loud during
the brief sermon response time about
civil rights and Central America.

Come to the lunch next Saturday
at the Holy Family Catholic Church,
they said, on Ponce de Lyon, for

a conference on the abuses of power
in Honduras, El Salvador, Guatemala.

Join us on Peachtree Street for the
civil rights march on November 7.

The elderly, some of whom had
taken a liking to young man Blaze,

voiced their concern for the
pastoral care which William T
did not carry through very well,

though they did persuade
him to call on Blaze at home.

The Charismatics, who met
privately to listen to the
tapes of other preachers,
wanted William T replaced.

Some said these tapes tell
what church must sound like.
Others nodded solemnly.

Blaze was there, and he said,
I am actually awed by William T
as poet and as pastor, and by his
cool, deft leadership of worship.

And he looked for a way
to leave the group. Yes,

William T's movements,
his manner, his gestures
of head and hands, in
the pulpit and at the table,

bespoke poem and prayer,
courage and depth of being.

The easy flow of originality Blaze
heard from the pulpit was subtle

and evocative, unlike what he was used to
hearing from philosophers at the university,
where one's publishing success was all in all.

This was important for Blaze Pascal,
who would never surrender such creativity
and freedom for the practice of religion,

which needed, he knew by now, to attract
minds of higher, not lower standards, and

sensibilities round and sharp to distinguish
between what is true and what is false,
between what is important and what is not.

And never had he heard,
nor had he expected,

such sermons and prayers,
with such style and grace.

Knowing intuitively that
he was in the right place,

the man of dust, now
the man with a prayer,
the man with a poem,

studied for a year with hospital chaplains
among nurses, therapists, and physicians.

The chaplains said,
Bury your essences,
tell your existentia.

So he suspended the rational during
his internship with the chaplains, and

let them teach him to console at bedside
in the downtown hospital of many floors,
above the sirens of perpetual perishing,

not with the truth but
with his own truth.

The chaplain counseled at bedside,
the philosopher returned to the cave,
and the bodhisattva walked
the back alleys of human suffering.

Then the man of dust,
the man with a prayer,
the man with a poem,

he fled from the pressures of the city,
dreaming of a lighthouse by the sea and a
singular church on the Naraguagus River
which had called him to be their pastor.

There in the old hemlocks the eagles and
ospreys built their nests in the summer.

A place of beautiful solitude
near the rocky cliffs of Maine.

Here he broke the bread
and poured the cup for

an excommunicated man,
watching the tears swell
and shine in his eyes.

It was here he stumbled and
fell, being vulnerable in love,

a need no one could answer,
for which he was unprepared,

which would become
his burden and challenge
for the rest of his life.

CVI

Blaze Pascal ate the forbidden fruit
of the knowledge of good and evil,

and forthwith hid in the garden
of the tree of moral knowledge.

There among the cedars and hemlocks,
fleeing from tree to tree, he was all alone
and no one came to befriend or counsel him.

He lived in a dungeon
for seven long years,
until he crossed
the wide Missouri.

It would be good,
the burden and the challenge
Blaze would carry forever,

as a lesson he learned
at the beginning of time,

as a lesson he learned
at the beginning of time.

Hang down your head,
O man of dust, you're
gonna carry that load,
carry that load forever.

And the man of dust,
who still had the prayer,
who still had the poem,

given him by the
person of heaven,

they kept him alive
for seven long years,

and they would keep
him alive forever.

Blaze P was a man of dust,
a man of dust with a prayer,
a man of dust with a poem.

A poem and a prayer.
A poem and a prayer.

Blaze P had a dream just three nights ago.
He was driving the family from Peshawar,
Sharif, Uzma, and the two-year old girl
in his car, all of them happy together.

Suddenly they found themselves in the
mountains walking on a snowy forest
road, not unlike the road he used when
he went to his cabin some years ago.

They came upon what looked like a
big lake or a river blocking the road.

The water was lovely, cold, deep, and
so clear that they could see the bottom.

A big log was slanting into the lake,
but they could not possibly use it to
cross to the other side, which was far.

There was nothing they could do
but to turn around and go back.

CVII

Blaze Pascal searched now for beauty like
the eagles and ospreys in the old
hemlock trees watched for the river to rise.

He looked for truth like the cranes on the rocks,
waiting for the blending of the river and the sea.

Not for perfect beauty,
nor for absolute truth, for
these are never found in
the world, only in word.

Though chords and colors send
intimations of perfection, and

sounds and textures
hints of the absolute,

the magical land lies not in
the world, nor in word, but
between world and word.

Not in the city, nor in solitude,
but between city and solitude.

Not in silence, nor in commotion,
but between silence and commotion.

The mystical land lies not in
sacred, nor in secular, but
between sacred and secular.

Not in flesh, nor in spirit,
but between flesh and spirit.

Half-truths pass at breakneck speed
from tutor to pupil in the Coyote Cafe.

No college nymph
grounds the man of dust,

the man with a prayer,
the man with a poem.

Only the hanging bridge
between freedom and love,
between hither and yonder.

Deep and swift is
the river below,
like the currents of
San Francisco Bay.

The girl with the black hair and midnight eyes
walks away with a strong young man with swag.

The waters crash and pound
in the chest of the man of dust,

the man of dust who is
the man with a prayer,
the man with a poem.

He walks uphill in the heat
to the seminary library and
the Garden of Ancient Trees.
He goes to write his lines.

CVIII

Darkness covers the deep.
Out of the void you come.
Obscurity does not become you.

Through the mist
you glimpse the beams
of the lighthouse.

The road snakes through lagoon and marsh,
the habitat of untold shrubs, ferns, flowers,
oaks, pines, cypress, deodar, and dogwood,

all manner of wild animals, rhesus monkeys,
langurs, panthers, jackals, pheasants, hawks.

You will hear the
double-noted hoot
of the Scops Owl.

At the Mulingar rest house you are
told, This is where the climb begins.

Strong sherpa guides
with Gurkha faces
carry your luggage

and take you on
rickshaws and hammocks
for a reasonable fee.

When you enter the city
some will look at you and
see the ninja in your walk,

and some will hear
the avatar in your voice.

They will test your limitations.

Practice restraint.
Protect your freedom.
Follow your heart.

The human world is growing.
The human world is growing.

CIX

A slender blonde had two children.
Her dancing enraged her boyfriend.

Last night he burned my money in the house.

Hearing this I lost my hold.
I grew weak and fell silent.
I saw the house go up in flames.

A dark pretty woman
gave me her number.
Seeing her the men swooned.

She promised cold pleasure,
but my heart was unwilling.

Loud liquid kisses a man did give her
up and down her arm on the dance floor.

They were up against the wall of mirrors,
visible to the other couples,
and she threw her head back and laughed.

I was glad for her:
She had scant love within.
Glum was her countenance.

The heart is existential.
It knows by intuition.

Deep in the bazaar,
near the ancient fort,
a crowd had gathered.

Some shouted, This way!
some shouted, That way!

I did not know
which way was true.

The voices grew louder
when the crowd
saw that I was afraid.

CX

Deep chimes came as Blaze Pascal,
the man of dust, the man with a prayer,
walked near the university and up to the
seminary and the Garden of Ancient Trees.

He knew Elsa Langley,
who lived higher up,

blessed by the sound of water streaming
down from the slopes of Contemplation.

He often thought of her
on his walks in this area.

She spoke of Rome and Jerusalem and Constantinople.

And how Angel City has grown, she said,
all by itself into this large luminous jewel.

Blaze was no match for them,
the smart, rich, cultured elite.

The Scarsdale party games required
quick minds and worldly knowledge.

He felt ignorant and odd with the family
gathering in the condo on New Years Eve.

In Seattle the loud wordplay
left no room for inwardness,
for deep calling unto deep.

Here he felt outsmarted
and outclassed by the
highbrow Hostetlers,

the parents and their
sons, daughters, in-laws,
on Thanksgiving Day.

He was quite uncomfortable and
felt excluded from the merriment,
and he left the gathering early.

Jonathon Hostetler himself,
in a passive but polite rage,
walked him out to the
parking lot in the dark.

The lights twinkled all around on
the shores of the big, beautiful lake.

Downcast he took the slow
route by the Arboretum,
closed at that time, and

over the Ship Canal Bridge,
into the University District.

Everything was closed on the holiday,
the pharmacies and grocery stores,
the Greek restaurant, Starbucks,
J.C. Penny's and the department stores.

He saw his car go by in the windows.
Suddenly he was on Market Street on a
holiday when he was a foreign student.

It was lonely seeing nothing in
the windows but your own face.

A big yellow moon gas station cast
its bright lights upon the misty night,
but the blue pumps drew but a
single car with woman and child.

She was cleaning the windows
hastily, loose hair flying in the wind.

He took a drive up Five before
returning to the big dark house.

No, he could never afford the country clubs, nor
had the money to invest in the local symphonies.

He was no connoisseur of
Western foods and wines.

He was a gluten-free vegetarian.

The contemplative simpleminded soul had
nothing to say, but the same thing over again,

Save the spotted owl and the
gray wolf and the grizzly bear,
the pronghorn in the Sonora Desert,
the wild lands and wild waters.

The wild lands and wild waters,
this he said with some authority.

CXI

Elsa was exquisitely beautiful
and had a doctoral degree.

She wore expensive clothes
and collected rare art from all
over the world, East and West.

A large painting of the Yosemite Valley Chapel,
dominated by evergreens and dark cliffs rising,

commanded the hallway to the dining room,
bringing old Blaze Pascal to a complete stop.

I was an assistant here, he said,
and read the scripture and said

said prayers here under the
Chaplain Michael C. Woodward,
when I was new in seminary.

Sixty years ago means nothing:
They are here now, the chapel,

the blue road, the reading of
theology beside the river and
watching the floats sail down,
the cliffs, the evergreens, the

teaching of the high school Sunday
School class under Yosemite Falls,

the college girl from Mississippi
and the Lebanese chef at the Lodge.

Elsa listened to Blaze in a
semi-meditative trance,
startled by his vivid images.

In the screened-in porch, in
the sound of roaring water,
she had said, No planning
made the promises come true,

this marvel of light,
this progress so bright,
this Disneyland night,

to be viewed from between the
moon and the deep dark sea.

No, he had protested, but from the hard surfaces,
the downtown realities of Broadway and Sixth,
and on the bridges across the freeway One-O-One.

Look at the lights at night
from the predicament of
human and nonhuman,

the look-alike housing and
the ugly warehouses and auto
and storage establishments,

crisscrossing freeways and
shopping malls and their
parking lots, all over the hills
and the former wilderness.

View the Disneyland night
from the point of view of the
autistic, extremist, agitated,

and addicted population,

shrinking the world unto itself,
flattening explanation, and
confining truth to its own prison,

perverting the soul's dark night,
practiced by magi east and west,

and turning a blind eye to the habitats,
migration patterns, and extinction rates
of species in the wild lands and waters.

Though they both know this
and still remain friends,
the gorge between Elsa and
Blaze Pascal is wide and deep,

like that between Glacier
Point and Yosemite Falls.

CXII

Blaze Pascal penned these
words after his visit with Elsa.

But I will be there, my love,
at Hollywood and Vine.

Let it be so for an hour
that all is left behind,

the autism, extremism, addiction,
absolutism, dogmatism, piety,
arrogance, contentment, denial,
exhibitionism, and ignorance,

the fragmentation and identity,
told by the man from Geneva,
the vulgar, the vernacular mind,

the agitation and the cancer, the
freedom without responsibility,

the terror and surveillance,
the detention and deportation,
 the ban, the wall, the ill-will,
the wars and rumors of wars.

Let it be so for an hour,

the fate of the grouse and the falcon,
the grizzly bear and the jaguar,
the bobcat, the prairie dog, the eagle,
the elephant, the rhino, the cheetah,

the snow leopard and the reed warbler,
the tiger, the blue whale, the bumblebee,
the beauty of river, marsh, and forest.

The good will surely
prevail at high noon,

 the right man will win
when the train comes in.

Where did it go, my love,
all that was meant to be?

The walk in the sand
at the break of day,

the place in the sun
overlooking the sea?

CXIII

It is good to step aside,
as a matter of principle,
for hikers coming down
the mountain trail.

The Chinese had hiking poles,
and the trail was narrow and steep.

Some had Sherpa faces, like in
Darjeeling, Ladakh, and Kathmandu,

and like the strong squat Gurkhas
who carried heavy loads through
Sisters Bazaar on Landour Ridge.

A Caucasian woman wearing a Kabul t-shirt
with a man hiked on uphill with a hardened face.

Was she wiser after Kabul?
Blessed are they who are

wiser after Kabul,
wiser after Baghdad,
wiser after Hanoi
and Dienbienphu.

They shall enter the gates of
healing and understanding.

Blessed are they who stand
on street corners for peace.

They shall know the truth
taught by John of the Cross
and Sakhyamuni Buddha.

T. S. Eliot understood these things
when he said to himself, Be still,
and let the dark come upon you,

meaning John's dark night of the soul,
meaning the Buddha's detachment,
meaning the cloud of unknowing.

Be still
and discern

the false hope,
the wrong love,
the bad faith.

CXIV

Time like an ever-rolling stream
bears its people and places away.

But they are not forgotten like a dream.
Daily they return, I hear their voices.

My father sits with me on
the Arroyo Seco Parkway.

We go to see Mrs. Dobson in Glendale
or Mrs. Shattuck in South Pasadena.

Or we are returning to the city.
The narrow parkway curves through
green grasses and meadows and golden
hills before crossing Angel River.

People of your past from
across the divide waited for you

by the old oak tree at the gate.

You were just a youth then.
Shyness washed over you,
the news made you tremble.

You had suppressed the hope,
which was less than hope.

Have they braved the
shadows of the ravine, the
boulders of the stream?

Or did they come the long
way, through the bazaar?

You know who it is that waits, but
your knowing is less than knowing,

and your joy is more than joy,
a private and unsayable thing,
on the stony road to the tree.

CXV

At an old fireplace and mammoth redwoods
overlooking the stream I sat down to rest.

The black soft soil,
the wind, and the stream
all called in unison,

Receive this food as your
prayer, your sacrament,
your dark night of the soul,

which is not without thought.
It is the mysticism of thought,

this hearing of the water and wind,
this perceiving of the soil, the trees,
and the incense in this sacred space.

Yes, what we hear,
what we perceive,
are not themselves
the depth of being,

but expressions of
the depth of being.

The intonations of the changing wind,
the insinuations of the roaring water,

the sisterly hinting of the incense of
times long gone and places far away,

they deepen our understanding
of word and wisdom,
and give us the courage to be.

We renounce the pride of fools,
rebuke the praise of the world,

and practice the yoga of the middle
path with humor and humility,

unconfined to this moment of solitude,
but blending it with life in community,
and in this way freely rising above it.

So I continue the dialogues
at Ground and the church,

and like the Rev. William T, the pastor
who gave a prayer to this man of dust,

who gave him a poem too to
tell the story of unseen things,

I write of life, savage, predatory, invasive,
ravaging the forests and grasslands,
the doomed habitats of a billion species,

yet creating beauty,
rejoicing in the truth,
marching for justice,
and reaching for love,

running down mountainsides, leaping
on boulders to cross streams, and

climbing up slopes on the other side
to kiss the girl we love and hold her
close in an abandoned place, all lit
up and fluffy, under the fragrant pines.

And consider these leaves falling around you,
answered the wind and the stream and the trees,

so fine their grains, just like the
lines of your grandmother's face,
the face you see in them now.

Time will pass.
Spring will come.

These very seeds in the ground of the
dead will not be lost, but
will burst the rock and possess the light.

The green blades will make their stand
against the wind and the blowing snow.

CXVI

No, I cannot live here and
resume such solitariness.

I had tried and failed, and
am now the wiser, humbler,
and aware of my limitations.

Yes, I loved my cabin, the
triangles above for the insulation,
which never did get started,

the beige brightness of the wood,
and the empty space, 30 by 30.

The fire in the stove, the
water from the spring, the
two joined Wal-Mart cots
with rug and sleeping bag.

But the silence of the night,
the isolation, the aloneness,
the stillness of the hours,
they began to frighten me.

Even the sun moved
eagerly across the canyon,
and the river swiftly
through the defile.

I drove all day, stopping
at the Columbia Gorge

to climb through the misty
spray up to the waterfall.

The quicker I got to Angel City
and the music and dancing angels

and the big boulevards and the
atmosphere in Contemplation,
the happier, I knew, I would be.

That night I slept in Rogue River,
walking along the river in the dense
old growth woods in the morning,

the next in Wauconda,
north of Sacramento.

Trucks and cars dotted the motel
lot. I filled up at the gas station.

Renaissance Gifts and Restaurant knew
nothing of vegan and gluten-free foods,
though they advertised home-made
fudge, candy, ice cream, and soups.

Their split-pea soup contained ham,
their potato soup was thick with cream.

I ordered a baked potato
with their tomato basil soup.

It was dark when I crossed
the railroad tracks
for a walk down Main Street.

The empty boardwalk creaked and
many buildings were shuttered up.

Turning right at a cross street
a light shone through
a window, and I heard voices.

Further down on Main a smallish grocery store
was well-lit and open and had a few customers.

The young cashier checked me out
in English. Walking through I had
picked up raw almonds and cashews.

The back streets were darker.
Huge oak and fig trees fronting
handsome old homes hovered
above me on the dirt road.

The alleys were empty too.

Outlines of silos rose in the distance,
ghosts of a grain empire long gone,
as I walked back to my motel room.

CXVII

Dialing for Sinatra and Torme
but finding songs that still say

I love you and Hold me close
in funk, Chinese, and Spanish,

I rolled the next evening into
the city I loved from the start,
even from before I first saw it,

the city of dreaming and dancing,

of Doris Day and Fred Astaire,

where stars leave their footprints,
and mortals cluster and collide
in clubs and cafes and colleges,

and feelings always run deep.
And feelings always run deep.

Stars or mortals,
they fall in love,
they get jealous,

they get deranged,
lovesick, or lusty.

They lose themselves.
Intoxicated they
try not to know.

It's not the flesh,
but the feeling.

The flesh is grass,
but feeling is word.

The giving, the taking,
the asking, the receiving.

It's not the finding,
but the looking-for,

the looking for some incarnation,
some messiah, some lofty thought.

The finding is soon forgotten,
the looking-for is remembered.

It's not the arriving, but
the climbing, the questing.

Time like an ever-rolling stream
may bear its songs away. But
they're not forgotten like a dream,
they await another day.

CXVIII

The climb has done us well.
We no longer feel the chill.

I no longer rush into things
which cannot be erased,
which torment me in my dreams.

I've learned to live
in my wrongfulness
and grow old in
my private knowledge.

The initial mistake is the
situation of our own doing.

The intention is good, but
the motives are unavowed.

Sin and creativity
in the same act, said
Reinhold Niebuhr.

The garden of the
knowledge of
good and evil is
the garden of power,

and power is a dangerous thing.
The serpent is coiled in the tree.

The same garden
of the tree of
forbidden fruit is
the garden of love,

and love is a dangerous thing.
Slithers the serpent in the grass.

They are inevitable, then,
the delirium of power,
the entanglement of love,
the consequences of the deed.

We cannot flee:
The world rises
up in mutiny.

And how can we
flee from ourselves?

CXIX

No, it will not grow dark again
as it did for seven long years.

They will not be taken
from us till we reach
the wide Missouri and
cross the raging water,

the cliffs, the cormorants,
the pebbles by the sea,

the snow owls in the winter,
the ospreys that made their
nests in the summer down from
the little white church on the river,

the same church that said,
Come away, come away.

Come away from the truth
of the waiting birds
that darken the world upon
changing to another rock,

the truth of the skinny
fox that crosses the
river for the farmhouse,

the truth of the bee
that falls silent in
the little brown
chapel in the woods.

Yesterday as grace I said,
May our bodies still be broken

for beings whose habitats
cross freeways and fences,
both private and public,

and our lives still poured
out for beings, injured,
abandoned, endangered.

I all but mentioned
the big Asian cats,
the blue whale,
the African wildlife,

and the jaguar
at the border.

CXX

The time had come:

Blaze drove to the City of Angels
to the Private Eye Piano Bar
to hear Julianne sing and look
for a chance to talk with her.

He went with trepidation,
afraid that he was forgotten,
fearing that she did not care
to talk with him any more.

But she flashed a broad smile his way when
she saw in his own handwriting his two song
requests, Easy Like Sunday Morning and Rainy
Days and Mondays Always Get Me Down,

and his request for conversation
about her visit to Pondicherry
and the Auroville community.

I want to hear your comments,
said the note, on Sri Aurobindo.

She joined him happily during her break
and told him of her admiration for the
ecological, interfaith, and humanitarian

emphases that the community exemplified,
and the mixed feelings about the mysticism
of Aurobindo's poetry and philosophy, which
she spent her time studying daily while there.

She spoke with him over the next three months,
a few minutes at a time, given the constraints
she was under there at work and at home.

Like the constraints, she said, of Satyavan's soul,
bound with rope by Yama, the fearful god of
death, in Aurobindo's poem masterpiece Savitri.

She invited him to have dinner with her and
Craig, her husband, and their two children,

when she could spend time at the
table telling the mythical story of Savitri
and Satyavan in the Mahabharata.

CXXI

It was a handsome three-bedroom house,
blessed with a spacious back yard and
shaded by a tall deodar in the front yard,
near La Cienega and Beverly Boulevard.

Julianne had already told Blaze about King Aswapati,
how in response to his endless devotion and prayer,
the goddess Savitri gave birth to a daughter and sent
her to be his own daughter, also to be named Savitri.

The young Savitri was so beautiful,
possessed so of radiant splendor,

that no king or prince asked for her
hand in marriage. Therefore she
had to look for herself for a mate.

During her search, she heard of the blind
exiled king Dyumatsena, who lived in the
forest with his son Satyavan, who as a child

loved horses and loved even to draw them
on the parchments that had been provided for
him by his father, who loved the drawings,

and how he now rode through the forest on
one of the horses they had brought with them
to their forest refuge. There were thirty of

them, but they had grown to fifty over the
three years they had lived in their new home.

Langurs and monkeys would
gather to watch the horses, but

the tigers and leopards had been
warned to stay away from them,
and when Satyavan went on his

forest rides along the myriad streams
that came down from the mountains,
at which the horses liked to drink, and

the soft clearings and meadows
through whose tall grasses and flowers
horse and rider would pass,

he would often see in the shrubs
and trees a flash of claws and
colors, which meant a leopard or

tiger fleeing into the forests of the rolling hills and
streams at the feet of the towering majestic snows.

CXXII

Savitri went into the forest and saw for herself:
Satyavan was a weapon of the living light, standing
tall and erect like a spear thrown by the gods,

a tablet of wisdom his brow, the joy of life
in his open face, which was as youthful as a
Rishi's and touched with light, his body a king's,
a lover's, imperious freedom curving his limbs.

Blaze was seated at the dining table now
with Julianne, Craig, his son Robin, and
Narindar, her adopted boy of seven from

India, as she picked up the story from there,
after her summarizing what had gone before.

Craig was handsome and
looked physically robust.

He had said the grace,
and Blaze noted his piety,
his use of Christian phrases.

He also noted Craig's politeness, and
that he had asked Blaze no question at
all about anything trivial or otherwise.
Blaze, however, made nothing of it.

And it was Craig who had cooked the dal soup
with kale and carrots and the gluten-free bread.
And it was he who had baked the apple pie.

Savitri came back and told the king
of the one whom her heart had chosen.

King Aswapati asked the heavenly sage
Narada of this Satyavan, whether he is

energetic, wise, courageous,
forgiving, magnanimous,
truthful, and beautiful.

Yes, said Narada, he is energetic
like the sun, wise like Vrikashpati,
brave like the gods themselves,

forgiving like the earth itself,
magnanimous like Yagati,

beautiful like the moon,
truthful like Sivi, and
generous like Rantideva,

with honor and rightness
seated squarely in his brow.

Does he have any defects? asked the king.
Yes, replied Narada,
sadly Satyavan is fated to die in a year.

At this a solemn silence fell upon the royal chamber,
just as a hush fell upon the faces at the dining table.

Craig, whose face till now had been expressionless,
even as he greeted their guest, looked directly at his
wife with obvious interest in what might come next.

Robin, who was said to be blonde like his
biological mother, bouncy and hyperactive too,
which did not favor his college grades, was now

perfectly still, his blue eyes fixed on Julianne.
He was such a beautiful boy, thought Blaze.

Narindar, sitting next to Blaze, had been
following the story carefully all along, and
now stopped buttering his bread in case
he missed what Savriti's response would be.

Blaze was moved by the sweetness of Narindar
and could not help but keep one eye on the boy,
absorbing his accent, his black hair and dark face.

Both Robin and Narindar had been full of questions
of Blaze about India and his birthplace, and
how he came to know and to like Julianne's singing.

Though a shadow had darkened Savitri's face,
continued Julianne, the tone of her voice was
firm and her face resolute as she reaffirmed that
her heart's decision about Satyavan was final.

Savitri went with her father's blessing to
her marriage with Satyavan in the forest,
which had been agreed upon by both kings.

True love was theirs,
based on the rightness
and wisdom that was

incarnate in their
hearts and minds.

But the year passed swiftly, and the
day that Savitri dreaded was four days
away, and she fasted for those days.

As the shadow of sadness darkened her
face, she followed Satyavan into the forest
the fourth day, saying it was to see the
blossoming of the rhododendron trees.

While Satyavan was chopping wood,
she saw him fall down in pain, clutch
his chest, and visibly gasp for breath.

It was then that the eight-foot, muscular, and fearful phantom
of Yama, the god of death, appeared with a rope in his hands.

An aura like lightning
sizzled around his frame.

His eyes were red like smoldering
embers, his gaze horrifying. He
seemed to look straight ahead of
him, not at anyone in particular.

It was the look of steely objectivity, with
no place for compassion or subjectivity.

Savitri rose and stood to face Yama,
expressing both respect for him as a
god and the determination to stand
by her beloved in the face of death.

It was clear that this would be a
battle between love and death,

and that Yama would need to deal with
Savitri if he was to take Satyavan's
soul into the black night of nonbeing.

CXXIII

Here Julianne stopped, saying that dessert
is coming up, and she would continue
the story after the pie in the living room.

Craig got up to pick up the used plates
from the table and to fetch the apple
pie in the oven, the ice cream from the
freezer, and the plates for the dessert.

Blaze asked Craig about his screenplay writing
and his substitute teaching at Hollywood High.

He told Blaze how one had to follow up
one screenplay success quickly with another
with the contacts one had come to make.

A rat race, he said, and the
competition is awesome.

He found the teaching more fulfilling, he said.
Much more creative because it means working
with kids directly to discover their strengths.

He sounded intelligent,
and decisive and diligent.

Dorsey, a kid in my class, is a superb track and field
athlete who has no inclination toward math and science,
though he's being pushed in that direction by his father.

But he loves stories, simplified versions of
Julianne's story. Would he not do better in

writing and the arts, or perhaps physical
education? I'm working with him and the
school to rethink the aim of his studies.

Substitute teaching, continued Craig,
also supplements our income. That
and the sale of Julianne's CDs help to
boost our miserable savings account.

Blaze also asked Robin about his college studies.
I'm going to be a veterinarian, he said, I love animals,
all kinds of animals, sea and air and ground animals.

I've loved animals ever since I was in kindergarten.
He giggled, My friends often call me Rockin' Robin.

Can I call you Rockin' Robin? asked Blaze.
Absolutely! I would love that, said Robin.

Narindar told him about his friends at Beverly
Elementary and his growing love for soccer.

His big brown eyes flashed with excitement as
he talked about his soccer and his new friends.

Everyone retired after dessert to the living
room anxious to hear the story's conclusion.

The apple pie was delicious,
and Blaze thanked Craig.

CXXIV

Yama saw Savitri following him as he
carried Satyavan's bound soul into the dark,
and he saw no sign of her backing down.

She spoke to Yama respectfully,
questioning his reasons for taking
Satyavan's soul when he was young.

Do not quarrel, said Yama, with a
decree predetermined and divine.

Follow the yoga of action, he said,
the world needs your magnanimity.

Practice kindness, do good works, and
you will forget your love and your grief.

Savitri replied promptly,
Who needs me now is Satyavan.
Who needs me now is Satyavan.

He needs my presence in death
as he needed my presence in life.

And it is part of my karma yoga to
stand before you now, O divine one,
imploring you for the soul of Satyavan,

that we may see that our good deeds
in this forest kingdom may prosper.

Follow, then, the yoga of devotion,
insisted Yama, and you will have no
time or energy left for grieving over
the death of your soul mate Satyavan.

O divine one, said Savitri, it was
in my very devotions, my chanting,
my offerings, and my prayers, that I
was led to the forest to seek Satyavan.

My duty to Satyavan is part of my dharma,
and my prayers to you, O divine one, are
themselves chants that I may use in worship.

Seeing that Savitri had answered his
arguments and admonitions so promptly,
Yama urged her to practice the yoga

of meditation, thereby to channel her
emotional energy toward divine things,
and thus to divert her grief into serenity.

Savitri said, O divine one, in meditation my
mental powers have been heightened and
directed to focus on what is right and good.

What I am doing now is right and good,
and it is the one thing I can do to channel
my grief into peace of mind and serenity,

to follow the soul of Satyavan
into the portals of death,
and die with him if necessary.

Yama was impressed by Savitri's wise
and prompt replies and tried one more
time to persuade Savitri to turn back
from the ghostly kingdom of night.

Practice the yoga of knowledge,
he said, knowledge will kill your
love and therefore your pain.

Not so! she replied firmly, and the sound
of truth was in her voice,
just as it had been in all her other answers.

Love and knowledge are like twins.
Love is the gateway to knowledge,
and knowledge the road to love.

To love the forest is to come to know the forest.
To know the forest is to come to love the forest.

Aurobindo tells how Savitri had fallen into the
abyss of loneliness, even from herself cast out.

She trod long hours behind the corpse of life,
lost in the blindness of extinguished souls.

But the moon shone bright that night on
Savitri's beautiful and godly countenance,

and she triumphed still over death:
Yama saw at the portals of nonbeing
the glow of her beauty, the fire
of truth, and the face of freedom.

He heard the voice of love, the mind
of justice, and the word of wisdom.

Yama heard at the mouth of the
cave the courage of being itself.

And noting her respect for him as a god,
he said, you may ask for any boon except
Satyavan's soul. She asked immediately
for Dyumatsena's sight, which was granted.

When she was offered other boons,
she asked for the forest to be kept
safe forever from the ravages of
human greed and exploitation,

for her own father to be given children,
and finally for her to have children of
her own, all of which she was granted.

But Yama knew that the last boon
required the release of Satyavan's soul.

She was therefore granted the soul of Satyavan
and a century of children with her beloved mate.

Then she turned away from the mouth
of eternal night, returned to Satyavan's
body, and rejuvenated him back to life.

CXXV

The great red sea of dawn
rose upon the forest,
waking all the animals.

The eagles circled in the sky,
the elephants blew their horns,

all the jackals howled,
all the owls hooted, the
woodpeckers strummed,

all the deer came forth,
all the apes emerged,

the big cats watched from
higher up in the rolling hills,

chirping parrots saturated the trees, the
peacocks strutted in dance formations,

and all the creeping, crawling, climbing,
all the running, flying things
rejoiced with dance and music-making
with tabla, singers, sitar, and strings.

When the fifty horses gathered to
greet Satyavan and offer him
a ride back to his waiting father,

so he could finally actually see him
and know that his son was still alive,

the handsome Satyavan stood up strong,
weeping out loud with tears of joy
and hugging each one and whispering in
their ears, for he knew them so well.

See how everyone loves you!
Savitri exclaimed to Satyavan,

who with his father had
brought grace and peace
to the forest kingdom,

protecting it from the rampant looting
and poaching of the earth and its
plants, streams, rivers, and animals
that had gone on before they arrived.

It was Satyavan who had guarded the
forest against the building of roads for
the exploitation of the forest's resources.

It was Satyavan who had negotiated a treaty
with neighboring kingdoms of peaceful
coexistence with his father's forest kingdom.

This, said Julianne, ending the
story with her own interpretation,

is how the Mahabharata
tells the big truth of spirit,

how love triumphs over
the shadow of death,

how the life of truth and goodness is
greater than fate and all the so-called
higher powers of the heavenly realm,

and how the courage of being must
prevail over the power of nonbeing.

From the corner of his eye
Blaze saw a cloud pass,
barely visible, across Craig's

face when he heard Julianne
tell the story's conclusion.

Blaze P thanked Julianne for having
invited him to their home to hear the

story. He thanked Craig for his hospitality and
for being the cook that he was. And he
thanked the two sons for their welcome of him.

He drove home with a heart full of joy,
glad for the love he had felt among them
and the hope he sensed about their future.

He wished he could understand Craig better.
He seemed to be remote emotionally, looking

at the world from afar, declining
to be touched, let alone moved.

Yet he was straight, like
an arrow shot by the gods.

A church-going man, albeit
with an uncritical theology.

He wondered what Julianne had meant when she
said she was constrained at work and at home,
like Satyavan's soul bound by the rope of Yama.

But he would let that lie. He
would not ask her to explain.

CXXVI

Blaze continued to go to
Private Eye to hear Julianne
play the piano and sing, not

just the old songs like I Cover the Waterfront,
Is You Is or Is You Ain't My Baby, and
Sometimes I Feel Like a Motherless Child,

but songs as recent as the Sam Smith hit,
Writing's on the Wall,
featured in the James Bond film Spectre.

A hush fell upon the club
when she sang that ballad.

All the James Bond songs were so
listenable, Skyfall, You Only Live
Twice, and From Russia with Love.

Goldfinger was so striking that
Blaze had been swept away by it
back in the 'sixties at the Chinese,

and it was what he remembered
most about the movie itself.

He also loved the way she sang the classic
Do You Wanna Dance, Hold My Hand,
giving it her own lilt and lure and love.

Do you wanna dance,
hold me tight,
kiss and squeeze me
all through the night?

Do you do you do you do you wanna dance?

Julianne would talk with Blaze for moments at a
time at his table. She told him about Narindar,
how she had come to adopt him. She described

her complex, hectic life with her family,
each person going his and her own way.

Blaze asked her about her church attendance,
knowing that Craig was quite religious.
She said that she too was a pastor's daughter,

and that she now goes to
Hollywood Presbyterian
to support Craig and Robin.

Even Narindar loves his Sunday School
teacher there, and Julianne often leaves
the sanctuary to drop in to the classes to
offer assistance to the teachers if needed.

When she enters Narindar's class, he
cries out loudly, This is my mother!

I find an empty room,
hide, and cry, she said.

And she shared her reservations about
Aurobindo, how he overshoots the mark

just when a spiritual guide must be
modest about what he or she says.

What is a spiritual guide for but to be a
light unto our path and a lamp for our feet?

I love the Savitri story as told by
the Mahabharata, she said, but
Aurobindo gets lost when he starts
making something more out of it.

Hermit-like he forsakes the world,
having the soul climb to impossible
heights never ever reached before,

breaking the bonds of death by
the simple denial of death,

flagrantly negating the driving
wheels of the engines of the
universe, the laws of nature,

defying the constrictions of
matter, ascending beyond

the world of desire and reason to
the ecstatic sweetness of Godhead,

and this through several layers, the
layer where the forms are revealed,
then to the forms themselves, next

to the absolute silence of the Self, and
finally to the presence of the Supreme.

These layers are supposedly beyond the
world, but are alleged to be actualities.

None of this is logical,
said Julianne, and is
admittedly beyond reason.

We are left absolutely worldless, with
no interaction with those around us,
let alone with light for our emergencies
and a lamp for our sombre hours.

The forms shoot through empty
space without bending low,
without epiphany or incarnation.

CXXVII

Blaze had come to like Julianne a lot,
though he knew to control himself.

He listened intently to her
comments on Aurobindo
and the modesty that must be
expected of a spiritual guide.

Was she talking in particular to me?
He asked this of himself repeatedly.

He seemed to fall silent in her presence,
as if she had become his spiritual guide,
as if she had some kind of claim on him.

Power and control still
ruled their friendship, but

it was a philosophical and mystical force,
it was a philosophical and mystical love,
it was a philosophical and mystical yoga.

She was popular at the Private Eye.
Everyone wanted a piece of her,

and Blaze often withdrew to a
table at the back or to the counter.

He saw her getting tired and needing
to disappear during her short breaks.

He saw her come and go,
taking turns with the other
clubs, so that he heard her
once a year for three months.

But her words still echoed in his soul,

*... always overshoots the mark just
when a spiritual guide must be modest...*

*What is a spiritual guide for but to be
a light for our path through the world?*

*We are left absolutely worldless...
the forms shine in empty space
without epiphany or incarnation.*

Blaze himself had advocated
a philosophical way of being,

a courageous way of being
a hermit recluse above the fray,
yet a hero in the thick of things,

a middle and immanent
path, a transcendent way
of being in the world.

The transcendence ensured
that we interact with the
abstract forms of goodness,

that we reach for the stars
and keep our ideals in view,

that we are not worlded,
corrupted by the winds of
doctrine, oppressed by the
pressures of circumstance,

movie stars strangled by fame,
rock stars poisoned by fortune,

broken into worldly fragments,
split off into worldly identities.

And the one foot in the world
meant that we still interact with
those around us, still benefit from
the beauty and love we experience,

still resist the violence that
darkens our path, still keep
our promises, and still offer

support and guidance in our
emergencies and sombre hours.

CXXVIII

Some keep their windows shut
and keep their curtains drawn.

They will not,
they cannot,
look outside
or interact.

They search, but
do not, cannot,
find what evil lurks.

A woman lived an isolated life, seldom
visible on the streets in the small town.

They knocked, and when she opened,
the darkness blew out like hot wind.
She held her gray pit bull with a chain.

A blue-eyed woman
sang blue-eyed songs
in a small church
on the golden prairie.

She couldn't,
she wouldn't,
sing Come Sunday.

It said O God of love,
look down and see,
see my people through.

See my people through.
See my people through.

A certain pastor was a hero, his
name was known far and wide.

People were talking.
People were talking.

He called meetings,
he held rallies, he
was a driven man.

In the meetings
he wouldn't,
he couldn't,

bear to hear
others speak.

His sermons?
Mediocre.
He had no time.
He had no prayer.

The people were stunned
to hear of his cancer.
And the cancer spread.
He didn't look the same.

Yama traveled to his door.
He was lying on the floor.

The cancer grows.
Extreme minds
mislead the world,

degrade the world,
teach false things.

They have no prayer,
no quest for truth,
no hunger for beauty.
It's the way they are.

Frozen minds
teach frozen things.

They will not,
they cannot,
hear you.

They have no prayer,
no loneliness for love.
It's the way they are.

Autistic minds,
ingrown minds,
teach identity.

Vulgar minds,
vernacular minds,
they teach
fragmentation.

They do not hear you
when you speak.

They have no prayer,
no reach for wisdom.
It's the way they are.

Loud minds
spread ignorance,
sow the seeds
of anarchy.

They do not hear you.
They have no prayer,
no thirst for justice.
It's the way they are.

Who will lead us now
in our emergencies
and our sombre hours?

CXXIX

There is no breakthrough into Platonic ideas,
no intuition dawns of a Brahmanic principle,

as what Schweitzer discovered
on a barge, surrounded by hippos,
upriver in the heart of darkness.

But the wild fowl and their chicks,
rummaging on the road, in the sage,
still transport the old soul to an
animated, guileless, luminous realm

of ecological wholeness,
human and nonhuman.

He still participates in the essential thing,
as did Schweitzer before the idea arose
of reverence for life, the bedrock principle.

The chicks we raised in the
old country came home in the
evening, at the end of the day.

In the savage beauty
of these pathless woods,
and the ghostly light
of the silent stars,

on this gravel road
from the snowy height,
who will stand guard?

There is healing too in
the reflections in the water,
and medicine in the ripples
and their widening rings.

Skirmishing birds do
inflame the situation.
They divert time, and
deprive the hours of
their slow passing.

But the depth folds the fury into
the trembling oneness of all things,

and holds out gently
to receive our sorrows.

ABOUT THE AUTHOR

Kenneth D. Stephens is originally from India, where he attended Christian missionary boarding schools in the Himalayas. He came to the United States to go to theological seminary, after which he went on to do his Ph.D in philosophy. His memoir *The Meaning of These Days: Memoir of a Philosophical Pastor* was published by Wipf and Stock. He is an active member of the African Wildlife Foundation, the Wilderness Society, and other environmental organizations, and resides on the outskirts of Los Angeles County.